RUNNING FAWN

SACRED GROUND

D.R. SMITH

Published by:

Light Switch Press

PO Box 272847

Fort Collins, CO 80527

Copyright © 2022

ISBN: 978-1-953284-70-9

Printed in the United States of America

CHAPTER 01

On a warm Spring Day, Smokin Peat was riding on his dark brown horse. He was checking the trail leading to the road the stagecoach used. He always looked for a fast and easy escape route. Once the stage arrives in town, the driver rapidly tells the marshal or sheriff. The marshal or sheriff is usually not too far behind them. Knowing the best trails to take made it easier for him and his men to avoid being caught. He came to a wide meadow with a few trees. He wasn't expecting to see anyone in the meadow. When he saw a red horse with a white blaze down its face grazing in the knee-high grass, he stopped his horse by a tree. He noticed the horse only had a blanket and bridle. Next, he heard a twig snap. He looked over toward where the sound came from. He saw someone kneeling on the ground. He dismounted from his horse. He tied the reins on a branch. The curiosity of who that person was made him want to know. He crept toward the person. He froze in his tracks when the person stood up. She stood still. They stood there staring at each other. Her long raven hair glistening in the sunlight was loosely in a braid. Two feathers on the right side of her head and one feather on the left side of her head with a wide headband holding them in place. Her buckskin dress went to her feet with matching moccasins. The fringes on the dress had beads. She was holding wildflowers in her hands. He looked into her dark eyes. He gazed at her medium build, cherry lips, and copper face. In the presence of her beauty, he felt ashamed of his appearance. He was rough-looking. A scruffy face with stubbles, dirty clothes, and pistols around the waist. His sandy brown hair moved in the breeze when he removed his hat. He had to somehow convince her he wasn't going to hurt her. She looked at the rugged white man staring at her. At first, she wanted to run, until she looked into his hazel eyes. She saw there was good in him. He didn't call her nasty names or try to grab her as the other white men did. She watched his average build walk up to her. He carefully tried to make his gruff voice soft as he said," Hi, I'm not going to hurt you. I think you're pretty. I hope you can understand me." Looking around it came to him she was alone. She surprised him when she replied," I understand. I speak your language." She did a sheepish smile. He softly asked, "What is your name?" Tilting her head to the left, she answered," I am Running Fawn and your name." Nervously he said," Smokin Peat, a Peat, just Peat." He smiled at her. He was smitten with this beautiful lady. He was lost in his thoughts about the two of them riding off together. He didn't hear her brother and other warriors coming from behind him.

When he leaned forward to give her a flower he picked, instantly he was tackled to the ground with a knife to his throat. His heart started pounding like a bass drum. It was the first time someone got the drop on him. In a pleading voice, he said," I didn't touch her. Please believe me, I didn't lay a hand on her." He could feel the cold steel blade pressing against his throat. The brave had Peat's arms pinned down by his knees. Peat swallowed hard. He was scared he was going to lose his life. He could hear Running Fawn and another brave arguing in their language. He sensed by the tone of their voices they were angry. Finally, Peat heard a familiar voice. I stepped my medium build down from my Paint to hopefully spare

Peat's life. I carefully said," Little Eagle, I know Smokin Peat wouldn't hurt your sister. I know him well, trust me. I will not lie to you." Peat let out a sigh of relief after the warrior let him go. The two warriors helped him off the ground. After standing up, Peat turned to shake my hand as he said," Thank you, Cali, you just saved my life." I could see the slice mark across his throat. I never saw Peat that happy before. Little Eagle walked his tall athletic build with long black hair flowing freely up to Peat and I. His dark eyes looked at Peat for a second. He calmly said," I am sorry if you are hurt, but we must be careful. The white man has tried several times to hurt my sister. She has been told many times not to be alone, but she doesn't always listen. I am her brother Little Eagle." Peat shook hands with him. Running Fawn rode away with a few warriors escorting her. Peat wanted to follow her. I grabbed his arm before he mounted his horse. After Little Eagle and the remaining warriors mounted their horses, he said," Cali, we will meet at the ridge to help bring in the cattle." I told him I'll be there in a few minutes. I watched them leave. Peat replied," You mind letting go of my arm. I would like to find Running Fawn to talk to her some more." I responded by saying," Running Fawn's father is Chief Eagle of the Cherokee Nation. He won't let you see her. If you try, they'll kill you and I won't be there to stop it. You were lucky this time. Leave, her go." I released his arm from my grip. We mounted our horses. He gruffly said," It's because I'm white." A look of disappointment was on Peat's face. He rode off in disgust. I could tell he was bitter about it. I rode to the ridge to meet Little Eagle and my ranch hands.

Peat tried to make himself feel better by thinking about the stagecoach's cash box. He met his men by the rocks near the road. They were preparing to rob the noon stage. They stayed hidden among the rocks and brush. They used bandanas to hide their faces. They watched the red stagecoach with yellow wheels being pulled by four horses coming up the road at a trot.

The driver, Casey kept the horses at a trot unless there was trouble, then a full gallop. Casey's husky build leaned forward slightly trying to see around the rocks and brush that may hide outlaws waiting to rob them. He was robbed once, not too far from here. He became more watchful than before for the outlaws. His brown eyes searched the road ahead. His shotgun, Georgia shifted his lanky build to get his rifle ready for trouble. His long mustache covered his upper lip. He pulled his hat hanging from the back onto his red hair. His blue eyes caught movement in the brush. He gave Casey a nudge. He pointed toward the brush. Casey started easing up on the reins to swing away from the brush. Before he could get the horses in the gallop, Smokin Peat and his gang appeared on the road. They had their pistols drawn. Casey brought the horse to a halt. Smokin Peat growled," Try anything, you'll be dead. Now drop the cash box on the ground." The one outlaw opened the stage's door with the pistol drawn. The two passengers on the stage were two older businessmen. Seeing the outlaw with the pistol pointing at them, scared them stiff. They had no guns to defend themselves. The outlaw ordered them not to move. Casey dropped the cash box onto the ground. Another outlaw dismounted to put the cash box onto Peat's horse. The outlaws quickly rode off onto a side trail away from the road. Casey urged the stage horses into a gallop to town.

Marshal Wil Bannon eased his average build-out of his office upon hearing the pounding hooves of the stagecoach's horses. He put his hat over his black hair. His dark eyes saw Casey walking toward him at a rapid pace. He had another feeling it was another hold-up. He gave his freshly shaven face a rub. Casey stood before him filled with anger as he said," Marshal Bannon, I have been held up. Those outlaws took the cash box again. This was the second time they held me up. What are going to do about it?" Before he answered Casey, he mounted his black horse. Sheriff

Mica and his deputy, Dusty rode up to Wil. Sheriff Mica's leathery face with a beard said," Wil, I talked to the stage passengers and Georgia. I was told by Georgia the outlaws took the trail off Cuttler Ridge Road. The outlaws wore bandanas and gloves on their hands. They didn't get a good description of them." Sheriff Mica shifted his stocky build in the saddle to see Deputy Marshal, Ty Barixa medium build with blonde hair walking up the street to meet them. Wil responded," Casey, Sheriff Mica and his deputy and me are going to look for those outlaws. Barixa, I'll need you to stay in town to watch for any trouble. We'll be back as soon as we can." They rode to Cuttler Ridge Road. Sheriff Mica saw the trail by the road.

As they started on the trail, gunshots were heard from a distance. They turned their horses to go toward the gunshots.

My ranch hands and I were moving 1,200 head of beef cows to the upper pasture. It wasn't easy to move 1,200 head of beef. We had to be on constant alert for rustlers. I noticed a rider on the hill. The rider wasn't close to us. I rode up to Rusty to tell him about the rider. Rusty was the foreman of my ranch, Diamond Rose. He was a grizzled medium build old man that worked for the ranch most of his life. His green eyes looked at me as he said," It might be rustlers getting ready to take the herd." We moved the cattle at a slow pace. My dark eyes scanned the hills for more riders. I wasn't your typical female. I wore pants and shirts to make it easier for me to ride and work. My father taught me how to shoot and ride. My horse, Duce was my birthday present from my parents a few years prior. I wore my black hair in a single braid. I readjusted my hat to cover my eyes from the warm Spring sun beating down on us. The chuckwagon driven by Charlie was behind us. He was an average build older man with hair of white, whiskers, tan skin, and a stickler about eating on time. I heard him shout," Cali, I'm going to start lunch up on the ridge by the tree." I shouted a replied," You might want to hold off on that! We may have trouble coming!" Upon hearing my response, he muttered," Dam varmints, don't they know I have a job to do." He eased the team of horses to the right to go to the ridge. He tied the team to the tree to start making lunch. He purposely moved slowly to the rear of the wagon to begin to make lunch. The first thing he did was get his rifle ready. He laid it on the wagon's rear board. Little Eagle and his warriors were watching the rider on the hill have four other riders come up alongside the other rider. I noticed my ranch hand, named Webb, waving his hat at me. I urged Duce in a trot to go to him. I rode up beside him. Webb was a scrawny build with a beard and lazy eye, said," I seen riders up on the hill, about five I counted. I think they're after the cattle." I replied," Ease the herd up to the right of the ridge. Have everyone get ready in case there is trouble." Webb and the other hands started moving the cattle closer to the ridge. I pulled out my rifle from the sheath under my saddle. The riders were slowly coming toward us. The number of riders increased by a dozen. I watched them cross the stream in a slow trot. I shouted," Everyone, get ready! Riders coming!" Rusty rode up to me with his rifle ready. Webb had his pistol in his left hand. The three of us waited for the riders at the stream bank. The riders stopped a few feet from us.

Dirty Birch Sayer average build sat on a dark horse. He had a shabby appearance with stubbles on his face. His dark straggly hair fell below his shirt collar.

His steel-gray eyes looked at me. The back of my hair stood up. I recognized his face from a wanted poster on a bulletin board hung next to my father's office. Dirty Birch Sayer was wanted for cattle rustling, bank robbery, and larceny. He has yet to be caught. He growled," I want the herd. Step aside or be killed." His men behind him drew their guns. They pointed their guns at us, waiting for the signal to shoot. Behind me, the ranch hands had their rifles out. It was a standoff. I saw his yellowish-brown teeth as he did a half-smile. He thought it was going to be easy to get the herd from us because he saw a female pushing the cattle. He was surprised by my response," You'll die trying. Now leave." Suddenly, Little Eagle and his warriors let out a blood-curling war cry up on the hill, causing Dirty Birch to whirl around. Instantly shots were fired in all directions. Everyone started to scatter. We were shooting at them as they were shooting at us. Charlie started shooting his rifle. Marshal Bannon, Sheriff Mica, and Deputy Sheriff Barixa arrived at a full gallop firing their guns. I saw Dirty Birch fall from his horse when it reared up. He was quickly picked up by his men as they galloped across the stream to get away from us. By the time it was over, five rustlers were on the ground dead. The remaining rustlers took off across the stream following Dirty Birch and the rider who picked him up. They disappeared into a cloud of dust over the hill. Sheriff Mica and the deputy followed behind them. Marshal Bannon stayed with us. He rode up to me. He asked," Cali, did you or anyone were hurt?" I answered," Pa, we're fine. I think it was Dirty Birch and his bunch. I remember the face from the wanted poster hanging by your office." I was grateful we didn't lose anyone. Little Eagle and his warriors rode up to us. They usually come to help move the herd and watch for trouble in exchange they would get four beef cows given to them. It was an agreement my father and I had with Little Eagle's father, Chief Eagle. His sister, Running Fawn and I was good friends. Their reservation was a part of the ranch's property. We agreed to give them five hundred acres to hunt, fish, and plant several vegetable gardens. Our parents were good friends. My mother, who was the town doctor treated everyone in the village. We heard Charlie ask," Is it alright to make lunch now?" I replied," Go ahead, we'll round up the cattle while you make it." By my father's facial expression, there was a mix of anger and concern. He calmly said," I'm glad no one got hurt or killed. I was out this way because the stage was robbed. Would anyone know anything about it?" When we responded no, we started rounding up the scattered cattle.

The upper pasture had a barn, bunkhouse, and coral for the cattle. We put the cattle found in the coral. Sheriff Mica and his deputy returned.

They followed us to the bunkhouse. They lost the rustler's trail. We heard Charlie ringing the triangle for lunch.

Smokin Peat and his men went to their hideout among the pines to divide the money from the cash box. It was an old log cabin that was abandoned. They would hide for a few days before robbing again. They decided the next place to rob was the bank in another town. Once the money was divided up, everyone went separate directions and would meet in a few days. Smokin Peat decided to get cleaned up and try to find Running Fawn. First, he would go to town for a bath and shave.

The town of Roaring Springs was bustling with people. They didn't pay any attention to Smokin Peat when he rode into town. He stopped at Barney's Barber and Bath House. The Silver Spur Saloon was next to it. A cross the street was the bank. Something Smokin Peat noticed. He decided to go into the saloon to get a drink first. He knew Sam the bartender from being in there before. He saw the saloon girls, Sally, Holly, and Lucky entertaining the cowboys at the bar. A poker game was going on in the corner of the saloon. Tobias was the dealer's name. A lady named Netti as usual was playing blackjack at another table on the far side of the saloon. The piano player, Jeb was playing a happy tune. Kati, the owner was a slender, tall brunette who made sure everyone had a good time but was well behaved. She didn't allow roughness, cheating, or stealing. She wore beautiful dresses and was polite unless riled by a bad customer. She greeted Peat warmly. He smiled back at her. The town drunk, known simply as Henry stumbled into the saloon to get his whiskey bottle. He was an older man with a bad leg from the Civil War. Being he had no family; Kati would let him use the storage room to sleep. To earn his whiskey, he did odd jobs for her, and she would give him a little extra money as did other merchants in town. He mostly swept floors and kept an eye on their stores. Smokin Peat finished his beer then went to get a bath and shave. He realized he needed new clothes for his bath. He walked across the street to the general store. He walked past Marcello's Jewelry store. He noticed the sparkling necklaces in the window. This gave him an idea. He also saw a bottle of wine on the jewelry counter. The man holding the bottle was looking at the bottom of the bottle. He shrugged it off as he continued to the general store. The owner of the store was Milly. A petite blonde with a bubbly personality. She smiled at him when he walked. She was dusting the shelves. He told her the clothes he needed. She helped him. Next, he took his clothes to the bathhouse.

Barney was slender small build thinning brown hair greeted him with a smile. Peat laid the money down on the counter. After a bath, shaved, haircut, and new clothes, Smokin Peat set out to find Running Fawn.

Finally, after searching for hours around the area of the meadow, he saw Running Fawn picking blackberries with other women. He waited by the tree for the others to wander away from her. She slowly crept toward him, not realizing he was waiting in the shadows. He quietly dismounted. He softly said," Running Fawn, it's me, Peat." She was startled to hear his voice. She looked at him. He said," I wanted to show you how nice I look. I shaved and put on some new clothes." She noticed his hair was combed and appear to be cleaner than the first time she saw him. She walked up to him. She brushed his cheek with her hand. He could feel the softness in her touch. She replied," You look better." He responded," I didn't know you were royalty, a princess." She asked," What is royalty, a princess? I do not understand." He answered," In my world, your father would be considered a King, mother, Queen, and the title of the princess would be you. Your brother would be considered a prince. The royalty titles mean you're honored, respected." She thought about his answer for a moment. She replied," We have no use for titles. Everyone has their place in the tribe. The tribal council is the elders, my father, mother, brother, and me. We all decide together for the tribe. Sometimes the Shaman help with the decision. You live in a strange world." They gazed into each other's eyes. He slowly caressed her face. She felt the tenderness. She softly said," I have to go now." He watched her walk away. She caught up with the other women. He mounted his horse. He slowly rode away. He didn't want to see her brother again. He was happy he saw her. He stopped his horse on a high hill to get a better view. He watched her walking across the makeshift bridge to her village. At last, he found her place. He started riding back to his cabin hidden among the pine trees.

The cabin was one room with a brass bed off to the left side. A wood stove with counter and sink next to it. A hand pump was connected to the sink to get water. A shelf of tin plates and cup were above it. A fireplace was in the middle to keep the cabin warm. A small barn with a corral was at the back of the cabin. The trees kept it hidden from view. It was a good hiding place.

During the night, Henry was walking past the rear of the Marcello Jewelry store. He noticed a freight wagon was backed to the rear door. He saw the crates in the wagon. He decided to take a peek at the crates. The one crate's lid was off. The crates were filled with bottles of wine.

He lifted a bottle of wine out of the crate to examine. He was quickly caught. He heard an angry voice say," Put the bottle back, now! You can't have it!" Henry put the bottle back into the crate. He turned around to look at the man who yelled at him. The man wearing a suit had a gun in his right hand. Henry carefully stepped away from the wagon. The man ordered him to leave. Henry slowly walked away thinking about the bottle. The bottom of the bottle felt different in his hand. He made his way to the Silver Spur Saloon to get his whiskey bottle before going to his room.

Sam eased his average build over to Henry. Sam's salt-n-pepper hair was combed back. Underneath his neatly trimmed mustache was always a smile. His brown eyes watched Henry take the bottle of whiskey he handed him. A smile and a nod, then Henry walked to his room. The room was off from the storeroom. A private room with a single bed, table, chair, dresser, and overstuffed chair by the window. Next to the overstuffed chair was an end table for the whiskey bottle and single glass. Henry put the bottle on the end table to take off his coat and hat. After he hung his coat and hat, he sat down in the chair at the table to eat his waiting dinner of biscuits and beef stew with a cup of coffee. Kati always made certain he had a meal. She seemed to understand his pain. When he finished eating, he went to the overstuffed chair. He let out a sigh as he sat down in the chair. He poured himself a glass of whiskey. He drank to forget the hell he went through in the Civil War. The whiskey made him forget the smell of gun powder and the sound of soldiers' screams from being shot. The most painful memory he wanted to forget was losing his family. He remembered he was just a boy when his pa was killed by cattle rustlers. He closed his eyes for a moment. He could see his ma working in the vegetable garden. Her long brown hair faded by the sun. Her once beautiful face was wrinkled from working long hours in the fields. His wife, Maggie did her best to help his ma. Maggie kept her sandy brown hair in a bun behind her head. He re-members brushing her hair before going to bed. Then the fever came in the Fall that nearly wiped out the town. First, his baby boy had a fever. Next, his ma had it. Maggie came down with it two days later. To make things worse the civil war started. Before going off to war, he laid to rest his wife, ma, and son within days of each other. The heartache was enough to break any man. He was quickly thrust into the ugliness of war. He remembered the severe pain in his left leg when the bridge exploded near him. The wood pieces pierced his left leg like knives. The soldiers carried him to the doctor on a makeshift stretcher. He was plopped on a wooden table made up of boards for the doctor to work on him. He was held down as the doctor went to work.

He shuttered at the thought of remembering that painful day. Another glass of whiskey to silence the torment. The shape of the whiskey bottle caught his attention. The wine bottle bottom was thicker and wider than the whiskey bottle. This puzzled him because something didn't quite feel right. He decided to talk to Cali about the bottles tomorrow. She would be in town to get the horses being delivered on the afternoon train. He agreed to work a few days for her. He staggered to bed, hoping to sleep peacefully.

In the morning, I rode to town with my pa and a few hands. A stock car of horses was coming on the one-clock train. I was to meet Henry at the blacksmith and livery stable. My hands rode to the holding coral at the train station. My pa went to the stagecoach office. He was determined to find the robbers. Quince, the blacksmith was working and pounding on a horseshoe. I dismounted from my horse. Quince was a mountain of a man with curly brown hair. His brown eyes glanced up at me. He said," Good morning, Cali. Henry's outback fixing a freight wagon's wheel for me." Henry already told him before I arrived, we would meet here. After I thanked Quince, I walked to the rear of the building. The freight wagon was propped up on wooden blocks. Its left rear wheel was off. I saw Henry working on the wheel. I walked up to Henry who greeted me with a smile. We exchanged hellos. Henry put the wheel down by the wagon's axle. Not saying a word, he walked up to the front of the wagon by the driver's seat. He reached into the wagon to get a bottle from the crate. He felt it was luck a crate of the wine bottles was left behind in the wagon. The bottle was empty. Henry handed me the ruby red bottle. I never saw a bottle that color before. He proceeded to tell me about last night. He softly said," The bottom of the bottle is different. You look at it while I finish the wagon wheel." I looked the bottle over carefully. I noticed a seam going around the bottle's middle. I gently pressed with my fingers to see if it was an opening. To my surprise, the bottle's bottom slowly slid off to reveal another bottom, only smaller. There was nothing inside the false bottom. I thought it was rather odd the bottle had a false bottom. I carefully put the bottle back together. I told Henry to return it to the crate. After he put it back into the crate, he secured the wheel to the wagon. When we heard a voice ask," Is the wagon ready? My driver is here to take it to the vineyard," we turned around to see Federico Marcello's average build with dark hair wearing a gray suit standing before us. His assistant's medium build with thinning gray hair wearing a tan suit stood next to him. Henry answered," Yes, it is." I devilishly said," Freddy, it's good to see you away from the winery." I saw Federico's face cringe when I called him Freddy. He retorted," I see your still playing cowboy."

His dark eyes were like daggers when he looked at me. I saw my pa walking up to us. Marshal Bannon said," Cali, your ma needs you and Henry's help." Not saying another word, we walked away from each other.

CHAPTER 02

Henry and I walked to my ma's clinic. She was Doctor Sherry Bannon, the town's only doctor. Her petite build with golden curly hair was packing medical supplies in crates when we walked into her clinic. Her blue eyes looked at me through gold rim glasses. She took over the practice when Doctor Ira Carter retired. He helped her win over the town folks. It wasn't easy for her. After a while, they became fond of Doctor Bannon. They called her Doc for short. Doctor Carter was finally able to retire in peace. He moved to Texas to be near his son and family. She happily said," I'm glad your both here. I need help to load the wagon. It's time to do my checks at the reservation. I'm looking forward to seeing Chief Eagle's wife, Morning Star. I was told Little Eagle and his wife; Yellow Flower is expecting their first child." I replied," He didn't tell me yesterday about his good news. The next time I see him I'll congratulate him. Ma, why would a wine bottle have a false bottom over top the existing bottom?" She looked at us with a puzzled expression. Henry and I explained about the bottle. She answered," There could be lots of reasons why it has a false bottom. If there is nothing in it, there is no need for concern." We took turns carrying the crates to the wagon. I saw Federico coming up the street in his fancy-covered carriage. The freight wagon being pulled by six mules with a burly driver in the seat followed behind the carriage, I heard the train whistle blow. It was time for Henry and I to go to the train station. Sherry climbed up onto her buckboard wagon. A thank you and then she was gone.

The Marcello family owned the local jewelry store and a winery located on the outskirts of Roaring Springs. Their local winery was the only one in the county that specialized in watermelon and strawberry. This made their winery unique. They lived in a vast stone mansion with the winery adjacent to their residence. Federico's carriage stopped in front of the mansion. The coachman opened the door for him. His assistant James Quintana, nicknamed Gin Bo, followed behind Federico as he stepped down from the carriage. James's favorite drink was gin and bourbon are the reason Federico gave him the nickname Gin Bo. The butler greeted them at the door. The butler informed them New York jeweler; Kye Thorn was waiting in the den. Federico recognized his short pudgy build with a white goatee and white thinning hair. He walked up to Federico. He put the satchel of jewels on the table. As he opened the satchel, he said," Mr. Marcello, I have the jewels you were expecting." Federico looked at the jewels Kye was holding in his hand. Federico said," Gin Bo, go get my mother. She is the jewelry expert."

Gin Bo excused himself to go get Francesca Marcello. He knew he would find her in the winery office.

The winery office was a large two-story building separate from the house. The winery store was next to the office building. He noticed customers at the store. When he walked into the office building, he walked across the polished wood floors that gleamed in the light. He proceeded up the oak spiraling staircase to Francesca Marcello's office. The double oak doors to the office were closed. He knocked on one door. A tall, muscular female with black hair opened the door. Gin Bo greeted Lynn Wyles with a smile and a nod. Lynn was Francesca's bodyguard. She was fluent in the martial arts and an expert marksman in knife and pistol. To say the least, anyone trying to get past her would meet their match. Zane Donoto another bodyguard for Francesca was medium athletic build with short-cropped brown hair stood up when he saw Gin Bo walk into the office. Francesca's slender build with dark wavy hair that flowed below her shoulders sat behind a cherry desk. She was talking to the family attorney, Christina Lauren who was standing next to her. They were talking about the paper in front of Francesca. They greeted Gin Bo warmly. Francesca removed her reading glasses. Her dark eyes looked at him. Christina eased her medium build with long blonde hair pulled back by a barrette, wearing a dark blue dress over to the bay window. The bird's eye view allowed her to see the property as far as the eyes could see. Gin Bo told Francesca about the jeweler. Francesca said," Christina, while I am with my son and jeweler, perhaps you could find a way to get the property from the rancher. I would like to expand the vineyard. The reservation is on good soil and it's by the creek. The property near the vineyard we already own but would like to expand to include the reservation land. It would give us a total of thousand acres extra to add more to the winery, however, there are the five hundred acres my husband purchased before his death has a story it's haunted. It's adjacent to the winery. Anyway, please try to find a way to get the land." Christina turned from the window to give her reply," I'll do what I can. I'll try Indiana Affairs agent, Adam Travis to see about buying the land." Christina left to try to find a loophole to buy the land. Gin Bo and Francesca returned to the house.

They walked into the den where Federico and Kye were still waiting for them. Francesca walked up to the desk. As she sat down, Kye laid the rubies and emeralds in front of her. She put the loupe over her eye to look the jewels over for any flaws.

Once she gave the jewels approval, Federico gave him the cash payment of $500.00. Kye put the money in a billfold. He said," I'll see you in a
month and it's good to do business with you. Both of you have a good day,
I have a train to catch in the next town." Gin Bo walked Kye to the door.
Francesca put the jewels in the safe. Federico said," I am going to check
on the property." She replied," I prefer to buy something built until we
purchased the reservation land next to it. Then we can expand the vineyard
at once." She reminded him about the stories the property was haunted.
It was, for this reason, her husband, and Federico's father, Tomas didn't
build anything on it. Strange occurrences happened that frighten Tomas
like a child in a storm. The materials to build would disappear to tools
being moved from one place to another. The workers would see someone
appear and disappear. There was screaming that made the workers run from
the site. No one could figure it out. From then on, the property remained
untouched until now. Federico blew off the stories. He felt he could get it
done.

The property was five hundred acres of rolling hills and trees. The green
grass was waist-high as far as the eyes could see. A stream ran through it.
The workers arrived with their wagons full of lumber and tools to start
building the warehouse and barn. The workers started staking out where
the buildings were going. A canvas tent was put up to be used as an office
for the foreman. On the table in the tent were the building plans. Another
canvas tent went up for the workers to eat lunch and take breaks. A breeze
blew through the trees. One worker walked up to the wagon to unload
the lumber. He was a scruffy build chewing on tobacco. His green eyes
caught a glimpse of something moving on the hill above them. He took a
second look. The image was gone with the wind. Picking up the boards,
he shrugged it off. Federico and Gin Bo arrived at the construction site.
The carriage stopped at the edge of the road. The coachman opened the

door for them. They walked to the office tent. The foreman's medium build with shoulder-length sandy hair was at the table looking over the plans. They exchanged hellos. They started talking about the warehouse being built first. The breeze turned into a strong wind. They thought a storm was coming. The wind started to pick up speed. The trees were creaking as the wind blew. Suddenly out of nowhere, a band of Indians wearing war paint on horseback came galloping toward them as they let out blood-curling screams. They repeated the word "AHIYALA!!" over and over. The horses were painted too. The workers scrambled under the wagons. The tents went flying in the air. Federico and Gin Bo with the foreman following behind them ran underneath a wagon. A few Indians had knives in their hands, others had bows and arrows. The Indians rode in all different directions chanting, AHIYALA. They watched the wagons shatter as the wheels burned to ash. The lumber was being twisted and bent. The tools were thrown in every direction. They were frightened. Some workers ran rapidly down the road. Some were too scared to move. Gin Bo shot at a few Indians. The bullets went through the Indians into the tree. He angrily said," I am shooting at ghosts, and I don't believe in them." Federico quipped," I'll get to the bottom of this. Someone is behind it." The foreman responded," We quit. Good luck, 'cause we're gone." He ran down the road as fast as his legs could carry him with the remaining workers following behind him. The horses pulling the wagons ran off when the harnesses fell from them. Federico's carriage and coachman went running down the road. The coachman was trying his best to get the horses under control to return to pick them up. They heard a long drawn out eerie strong voice in the wind saying," S-A-C-R-E-D G-R-O-U-N-D!" The voice repeated the words several times. Federico's carriage returned for them to get in. The horses were fighting the reins. Once they were inside the carriage the coachmen had the horses go in a full gallop. Their nerves were rattled. All at once, the

Indians vanished with the wind. Everything became calm. Gin Bo put his gun in the holster. They sat up in the seat of the carriage. Federico for the first time was rattled by what he saw. He had to take a breath to collect his thoughts. His voice quivering said," Someone is behind this because they want the property, or this is real. If it is real, we are in big trouble, cause I don't know how to get rid of ghosts." Gin Bo replied," I saw the Indians vanish into thin air or maybe it's my imagination. I think I need a stiff drink. Maybe my eyes were playing tricks on me." The carriage arrived in town at a fast pace.

Marshal Bannon approached the carriage when it finally stopped at his office. He opened the door to see Federico and Gin Bo shaking and ghost-white pale. By appearance, they looked frightened. He helped them out of the carriage. After they sat down, they told him what happen. Marshal Bannon said," When you get calmer, we'll go out there together to see what happened. I'll have Sheriff Micca go with us." He gave them each a cup of coffee. Deputy Barixa walked into the office. He told him about the workers and what they have seen at the property. The workers were at the Silver Spur getting their nerves settled down.

Marshal Bannon and Sheriff Micca arrived at the property. They rode around the twisted and bent lumber. They noticed the wagons were de-stroyed with the hand tools scattered in every direction. Shortly thereafter Federico and Gin Bo arrived in the carriage.

Federico angrily said," Marshal, as you can see there is damage all around and I want the person responsible arrested. Those Indians left the reservation to attack us. I want the person who helped them to do this to pay for the damages." A slight breeze blew across the trees. Marshal Bannon looked up to see a warrior sitting on his horse. In a blink of an eye, he was gone. Sheriff Micca responded," I think my eyes were deceiving me. Did you see a warrior on the hill?" Marshal Bannon became uneasy. He didn't want to believe what he saw. He kept telling himself there was an explanation. He carefully answered," I know the Indians were helping Cali with the herd. I think I know of a person that may have the answer to what happened." Sheriff Micca noticed a body by the stream. He rode over to it. He shouted, "Marshal Bannon over here." A dark-haired man with a beard wearing a suit had his head resting on a rock. Sheriff Micca dismounted from his horse. He checked for a pulse. Marshal Bannon rode up to him. He said," Micca, that's Indian Agent Adam Travis. What would he be doing out here?" He answered," The man is dead. He may have hit his head on the rock. I'll go get a buckboard to take him to town." He mounted his horse. He rode back to town.

My hands and I were out checking the fence line for openings. When I came up the ridge, I saw my pa, Federico, and Gin Bo looking around the property. It looked like a tornado ripped through the property with pieces of wood scattered everywhere. A rustle of the leaves in the trees caught my attention. I looked up to see a warrior sitting on his horse. He vanished before my eyes. I thought for a second, I was going to faint. I heard a soft voice say," They were here," which caused me to jump two feet off the saddle. I was startled and at the same time glad to see it was Running Fawn behind me. Riding his horse beside her was the Shaman, Wise Owl. In a shaky voice, I said," I saw a warrior on the hill over there." Watching the activity below us she replied," The spirit warriors protect the land. A man wanted this land. The government gave it to us. The man had men come to the village to scare us away. The warriors fought back. The ground bleeds red. Many warriors died. The government took the land from us. The man got the land." Wise Owl responded," The spirits will not rest until the wrong that was done become right. The man wanted the woman with flaming hair and eyes of the sky. Her name was Elly. She came to the village to teach us to read and write English to understand the English world better. Strong Bear and Elly fell in love. The man became angry she chose to stay with Strong Bear. Strong Bear and Elly had a son, Little Bear. Strong Bear called him Cubby. He had flaming hair and eyes of the sky like Elly. She was given the name Honey Bear.

The man sent men to the village during Springtime. The warrior you see alone is Strong Bear looking for his wife and son. He was killed protecting them. They disappeared from the village. We were forced to move from the land. The man got the land. An agreement between your father, Chief Eagle, and the government let us move to the land your father gave us. An agreement between friends." They started riding toward their village. I continued checking the fence line.

Running Fawn decided to check the fish traps with the other woman and her mother. The fish traps were made of strong vines. The bait was placed inside to lure the fish in, but not able to get out. The fish traps were placed alongside rocks and banks of the creek. Peat saw her by the rocks, out of sight from the other woman. She was bent down trying to free the fish trap without losing the fish. He startled her when he came up beside her. They looked at each other. When their hands touched the trap together, a rush of feelings went through them. He wanted to kiss her but he was to shy do it. He was afraid it would make her run away from him. They stood up still holding the fish trap. She gently said," Peat, you can let go. I can carry it from here." Releasing his hand from the trap, he replied," I'm happy to help you." They smiled at each other. He helped her to her horse. Once she was mounted, he gave the fish trap to her. He watched her ride to the village.

Smokin Peat rode to meet his men at another town. They were going to rob the bank in the morning. They would camp nearby to get ready. Peat always robbed banks in the morning, shortly after the banks opened. The morning meant fewer people in the streets, making the escape easier. When morning came, they rode into town. Two outlaws remained with the horse. Peat and the others stormed the bank with guns drawn. Peat threw the saddlebags on the counter. He snarled," Fill the bags." The two older women customers stood against the wall scared stiff. The two tellers quickly filled the saddlebags. They were trembling as they removed the money from the drawers. Once they were finished, the tellers put their hands up. Peat and another one of his men grabbed the saddlebags. As they were leaving Peat grabbed an older woman, lower his bandanna, and then quickly kissed her on the lips. This shocked the older woman. Peat pulled the bandanna up to cover his face. In a few minutes, they were gone. The one teller ran out the door shouting for the Sheriff. The bank manager ran out of the general store. The Sheriff and two deputies ran into the bank. The Sheriff started asking questions. The bank manager walked in. When they asked for the description, the older woman said," He kissed me. I couldn't believe it."

She was still shocked it happen. She couldn't describe the outlaw except his lips taste like coffee. The Sheriff and his deputies went in the direction the tellers told them. They gallop their horses to the outskirts of town. They lost their trail a mile away. The Sheriff put a wire out about it. Peat became known as the kissing bandit.

Marshal Bannon went to the reservation. He wanted to see Wise Owl. He saw his wife, Sherry treating Yellow Flower because she was due to have her baby any day. They gave each other a wave. He saw Wise Owl sitting beside Chief Eagle. He said," O'siyo Oginalii." Translated it was hello friend in Cherokee. Wise Owl and Chief Eagle said the same words to him. They offered him to sit down. Marshal Bannon told them about the unusual activities at the property next to their reservation. Wise Owl said," Bannon, the spirits will not rest until the truth about the land is told. The land was taken from us. I cannot answer about the Indian Agent's death. He was not a good man." Chief Eagle agreed with Wise Owl as he replied,"

He would meet a man in fancy clothes by the creek. They were talking and pointing their hands toward us. They did not want us here. They wanted this land, too. Fancy clothes are greedy. The Indian Agent was helping Fancy Clothes." Bannon asked," Did anyone see the Fancy Clothes man?" Wise Owl answered," Yes, he was here. You were with him. Tin Star took Indian Agent away on the buckboard." Tin Star was a nickname for Sheriff Micca who respected them and they, in turn, respected him. Bannon had an idea who the man was. The next question is why he and the Indian Agent were here before now. He excused himself. He walked over to his wife. Sherry was talking to Yellow Flower. Bannon softly said," Pardon the interruption Yellow Flower, but I need to speak to my wife." Yellow Flower replied," I understand. It's time I go for my walk with Morning Star and Running Fawn." When the three women were out of sight, Bannon asked," Did you get a chance to look at the Indian Agents Body?" She answered," I did this morning before coming here. There are no injuries to the head or anywhere on his body. He may have been frightened to death. Morning Star told me the spirits were upset yesterday and she noticed they have been making their presence known by causing the wind to be stronger than usual. Is there something going on?" He replied," I'm going to check the land office about the land next to here. I have a feeling the Marcello family is somehow involved. I must send a telegram to Indian Affairs for another Agent. I only hope the next one is better than the last one. Please be careful. I think the trouble is brewing." She responded," I'll be here until Yellow Flower has her baby. I don't want anything to go wrong. The town will send someone if I am needed." They gave each other a quick kiss goodbye. He returned to town.

Marshal Bannon arrived at the telegraph off before going to the land office. Agatha greeted him with a smile. She was sorting the mail. Her reading glasses hanged around her neck by a gold chain. Her neatly graying hair was combed back in a braid. Marshal Bannon said," Agatha, I need to send a telegram to Indian Affairs for another Agent. Their present Agent passed away unexpectedly." She put on her reading glasses as she wrote down the message he wanted to send. She replied," I'll send the telegram right away. I'll let you know when they send an answer." A quick nod as he started walking to the land office.

At the land office, Marshal Bannon saw the land clerk at his desk working on a map. Standing his average build-up, he said," Good afternoon, Marshal Bannon. What can I do for you?" He pushed his sandy blonde hair back with his fingers as he walked up to the counter. Marshal Bannon answered," Harold, I want information on the property by Willow Creek. The property is under the last name Marcello. I want to compare it with my ranch's property lines. There is something that doesn't quite feel right. While you're looking, check all the property belonging to Marcello." Harold replied," It's going to take some time. Are you in a hurry?" He responded," I'll be back tomorrow afternoon." Harold started to go through books and the file cabinets for present and past deeds. He laid the county map with property lines marked on the table. As Marshal Bannon was leaving, Harold said," Wait a minute. You need to look at this." He walked up to the map Harold had on the table. Harold pointed to Willow Creek. The property lines of the ranch went to it. The book-entry didn't match the map. Puzzled, Harold said," I'll request a surveyor to check the lines, but the book-entry has it a part of your ranch. I'll check other maps and entries of past years." Marshal Bannon asked," When can you have a surveyor here to do it?" Harold replied," I'll send a telegram to Emmett Graff. He's the best surveyor I know. I'll let you know when he'll be arriving." Marshal Bannon responded," It's a possibility the deed to the land isn't Marcello's." Looking through the deeds Harold said," The deed may be a fake, but I'll keep searching and verify with the surveyor." Marshal Bannon thanked him and then left.

The General store was busy customers when Morning Star, Running Fawn, and Brave Wolf walked in with their jackets, moccasins, handbags, and beaded bracelets to sell in the store. Milly had a section for their items to sell. They never wanted money. An agreement between them was that they receive supplies in exchange for their leather goods. Milly sold their stuff easily with the travelers coming and going.

The customers stopped their shopping to watch Milly and Morning Star exchange supplies. Milly said," Morning Star, everything has fine crafts-manship. I especially like the jackets with the fringes and beads. A good eye for details. Now, tell me what you need." I walked in with my hands following behind me. Milly saw me. She told me she would be with us in a minute. Milly gave them crates of food and blankets. As they were leaving, I said," Morning Star, I can drop off your supplies on the way home. It'll be easier than trying to take it on horseback." Smiling, she said," You are a good friend. For your help, please take the jacket." She handed me a buckskin jacket with fringes and beads. I accepted with a smile. I replied," I thank you. I'll drop off your supplies after I get a few rolls of barb wire." She gave me a nod. I watched them ride away. The customers resumed their shopping. My hands started loading the wagon with their supplies and barb wire. Federico and Gin Bo were watching the activities at the store. They walked up to us as we were leaving. I could see the anger in their faces. Federico growled," Those savages trespassed on my land and attacked us. You and the storekeeper doing business with them is insulting. Both of you should be horsewhipped." I snarled," They are not savages, you are." I went to mount my horse, but Federico grabbed my arm. I instantly slugged him hard as I could right square on his jaw. He dropped to the ground like a sack of potatoes, out cold. Gin Bo started shouting for the

Sheriff. Everyone came all around us. Marshal Bannon and Sheriff Micca came running. They quickly told everyone to move on. By now Federico started to come awake. He staggered onto his feet. He breathlessly said," I want her arrested." They looked at me. Milly said," Sheriff, Marshal, he grabbed Cali's arm, and then she hit him. Federico was mad because he saw Morning Star doing business with us." Speaking in a stern voice Marshal Bannon said," She was defending herself. If you ever touch my daughter again, I'll arrest you for assault. Now get moving." We watched them walk toward their carriage. I finished mounting my horse. The hands were on the wagon waiting to leave. My pa and I looked at each other. Grinning he said," I'm glad to see my daughter can handle herself. I'll see you tonight." I replied," You taught me well. I'll see you later," with a nod my hands and I rode toward the reservation.

Agatha saw Henry sweeping the train station's platform. She would pay him to sweep it twice a day. She called to him from the window. When he walked up to her, she said," Go tell the Marshal I have an answer to his telegram and let Harold know he has one too." Henry walked to the Marshal's office first.

He found the Marshal sitting outside of his office talking to Sheriff Micca. Henry said," Marshal there is a telegram for you at the telegraph office." After Henry gave him the message, Henry walked to the land office. Harold had papers laid out everywhere with file drawers open when Henry walked in. Once Henry gave him the message about the telegram, Harold quickly locked up the office to retrieve it. He and Henry walked to the telegraph and train station at once. Marshal Bannon was reading his telegram about the new Indian Agent arriving in three days. Agatha gave Harold his telegram. He was relieved to read Emmett would arrive at the beginning of next week. Harold said," Marshal, Emmett will be arriving the following Tuesday. I am looking forward to his arrival because there are several discrepancies I

discovered. I can better explain when he comes." Marshal Bannon replied,"
Good, I look forward to getting it settled. Agatha, while I am here there is
another telegram I would like to send." Agatha met him at the window with
pencil and paper in hand. He said," Send to Judge Ward. Come immediately, because a land dispute is about to surface." She wrote down his request.
Harold returned to the land office. Marshal Bannon mounted his horse to go
to the reservation. He wanted to inform Chief Eagle about the new Indian
Agent coming. At that very moment the editor of the town paper, Roaring
Springs Gazette, Dottie was at the train station to get the train schedule.
She overheard the conversation and became curious. She quickly removed
a pencil from her auburn hair. She walked her lanky build-up to Marshal
Bannon's horse. She removed her tablet from her handbag. Looking up at
him she asked," Marshal, what is the story about the land dispute?" She
put her wire-rim glasses on. She stood there staring at him with her hard
gray eyes waiting for an answer. He thought for a moment. He shifted in
the saddle. He asked," Dottie, can you ride out with me to the reservation?
There is something I would like for you to see." She eagerly replied," I'll
go get my buggy and be with you in a few minutes." They rode together to
the reservation.

CHAPTER 03

Marshal Bannon dismounted at Chief Eagle's house. Dottie stepped out of her buggy. Wise Owl walked toward them. Marshal Bannon introduced Dottie to them. He said," Dottie, this is Tyee Wohali, meaning Chief Eagle and Agatanahi Ugugu translation, Wise Owl. I would like your permission to show Dottie, Wahkan Gadohi, sacred ground, and explain it to her. Wise Owl, I may need your help with the spirits. They may get upset if we walk on it. Would you come with us?" Wise Owl replied," The Great Spirit can only control the spirits. I can not. I will go with you to calm them." Chief Eagle responded," You may go and find the truth for it has been hidden too long. May Wise Owl and the spirits help you on your journey to find the truth." They walked across the bridge over the creek to the land.

The wind slightly blew through the trees. Wise Owl raised his arms with hands flat out like he was trying to touch the sky. He said," Great Spirit, we come in peace. We ask you to help us on our journey to find the truth for all to see." Dottie was interested, yet a little scared. This was something she had never seen before. She saw the devastation of the wagons and lumber. She noticed the tents were torn in shreds. She asked," What happen here?" Marshal Bannon answered," You have to know about the past to understand the present." Pausing for a moment to sit down on a log. He continued speaking," The Cherokee named this place Wahkan Gadohi. It means sacred ground. The wind that blows across this place is called Tanamara. It was about ten years ago Tomas Marcello came to Roaring Springs to open a winery. He and his brother owned a winery in New York. His brother used grapes to make wine. Tomas wanted to use watermelon and strawberry. The reason he came, he heard there was good farming soil here. He bought 740 acres of land. Being he came with plenty of cash to get started, men went to work for him quickly. He built his house, buildings, and started the vineyard. He was so busy the first year he was here, he didn't notice the reservation until the following Spring. He returned to New York late Fall. In late Spring, he returned to Roaring Springs to open his winery shop. This land we are sitting on was the reservation. He became interested in it because of the water and good soil. One day he went to the general store to get supplies. He saw a young woman with long red hair getting a few things. He took a strong interest in her, not knowing she was married to a warrior and the teacher living on the Cherokee reservation to teach them to speak, read and write English at the request of Chief Eagle who wanted to learn English to better understand our way of life.

She taught the children and adults. Her name was Elly Atler. Ulanigida Alisoqualvdi meaning Strong Bear was the warrior who fell in love with Elly, and she fell in love with him. They were married by the Cherokee ceremony and their son was nine by the time Tomas came here to Roaring Springs. The next time Tomas saw Elly, he approached her, but she told him she was married to Strong Bear, and they have a son. Tomas told her to leave that life behind because she was white and should be with a white man. He became demanding. Tomas became angry when she refused to go with him. She told him she was in love with Strong Bear and would never leave him for anybody. Tomas hired men to scare them off the land. Indian Agent Travis believed Tomas about his men being attacked by the warriors. Somehow Tomas was able to buy the land and Chief Eagle and his people moved to the land I gave them. During the attack, Strong Bear and several warriors were killed along with several of Tomas's men. Elly and her son disappeared. Nobody knows what happens to them. There are stories about the land being haunted. It is protected by the spirit warriors. As for Tomas, his wife and half-grown son arrived from New York a month later. None of us knew he was married or had a son. We were surprised when they step down from the train asking about him. I showed them to his house. Shortly thereafter they opened the jewelry store in town. Tomas passed away from the fever that swept through the town a few years back. Federico, their son is grown and running the winery. The new Indian Agent will be here in a few days and the surveyor will be coming next Tuesday. I want you present during the surveying." Dottie became curious about the Cherokee marriage ceremony. She asked," Wise Owl, could you explain the marriage ceremony because I have never seen or been to a Cherokee wedding ceremony." Wise Owl answered," It is a sacred day for two people to become one before the Great Spirit. There are several steps they must do before the day of the sacred ceremony. They plant a flower or give each other flowers. It is for the love growing between them. Secondly, they make a windchime together for the harmony and music their love makes in their heart. Thirdly, they do seven steps around a ring of fire as they say seven vows to each other. The seventh vow is said together when they have met in the middle of the circle. Everyone stands outside the circle during the seven steps. The circle is the sacred hoop. The fourth step is done on the day of the ceremony. They wash each other's hands in holy water. They are washing away the past to start their new journey together. They each wear a blue blanket at the ceremony. I say a wedding prayer. After they say their vows to each other, the blue blanket is replaced with one white blanket. I wrapped them both in the one white blanket to begin their new journey together."

Dottie asked," What is the wedding prayer?' Wise Owl was pleased she was interested in learning their traditions. He replied," I'll tell you the prayer. Great Spirit, please protect the ones we love. We honor all you created. We come to you to unite two hearts and two lives together. Honoring Mother Earth, may their marriage grow strong all seasons. Honoring Fire, may their hearts glow with love as their union keeps them warm. Honoring Wind, in the Great Spirit's arms may they sail through life calmly and safely. Honoring Water, may their hearts never thirst for love. Great Spirit of all forces we pray they have harmony, true happiness, never-ending love for each other as they grow forever young for eternity; Aho." Dottie responded," You have a beautiful wedding ceremony. It is very touching." A slight wind blew across them. They looked up the hill to see Strong Bear sitting on his horse. Wise Owl said," Ulanigida Alisoqualvdi is still waiting for his family." The wind blew again and he was gone. Dottie wrote down everything told to her. Once she had all the information, she'll write the story for the paper. They returned to the reservation to leave.

Henry was on his usual late-night walks. The crescent moon was shining above. He decided to walk behind the jewelry store again. He wanted to see if the wagon was there. Once he saw it, he crept up to it. He looked inside the bed of the wagon. The wine crates were filled with bottles of wine. He carefully removed a bottle close to the driver's seat. In its place, he put an empty whiskey bottle. He placed the wine bottle under his coat. He quietly slipped away. He went straight to his room. He quickly hid the wine bottle in his bottom dresser drawer under his shirts. He knew he had to get to the Silver Spur Saloon before Sam start sending one of the girls to look for him. When Henry walked into the saloon, Lucky noticed Henry was shaky.

She walked up to him. She asked," Henry, is there something wrong? You seem to be not your usual self." Sam sat down a shot of whiskey in front of him. Sam replied," You're a little later than usual. Have a drink on me." Henry responded," It's one of those nights that I feel a little off. I get my whiskey in me, and I'll be fine." He didn't want to tell them what he did. He never took anything in his entire life until now. This rattled his nerves. He wondered how outlaws do it. He drank his shot of whiskey straight down. Sam gave him his bottle of whiskey. After Henry picked up his bottle of whiskey, he thanked Sam for the drink. He returned to his room to eat his dinner. He decided to take the wine bottle to Marshal Bannon in the morning.

New dawn meant Smokin Peat and his gang were robbing another bank in another town. The bank manager didn't expect anyone coming up from behind when he went to open the rear door of the bank. The one day he decided to go in earlier to review loan applications, he's robbed. Nervously he opened the rear door. A female teller walked up to the door to help him was quickly whisked in. Peat threw the saddlebags on the desk. He growled," Fill the bags. Try anything, I'll drop you where you stand." The manager and teller filled the bags with shaky hands. The two outlaws grabbed the bags once they were filled. Peat grabbed the teller around her waist. He held her tightly to him. She couldn't believe this was happening. Peat ordered the manager to face the wall. Once the manager had his back to Peat, he pulled his bandana down and kissed the teller on the lips. This shocked the teller. Peat released his grip on her as he ran out the door. He put the bandana back on his face. They swiftly galloped away. The teller stood there in disbelief. The bank manager turned around. He ran out the door to get the Sheriff. They returned with a posse. The Sheriff asked her to describe his face. All she could say was he kissed me right on the lips. They rode off hoping they catch them before the trail became cold.

When Henry woke up, he removed the wine bottle from the dresser drawer. He walked to Marshal Bannon's office. Deputy Barixa offered him coffee and eggs. Henry accepted with a nervous smile. Marshal Bannon asks," Henry, is there something I can do for you?" Henry placed the wine bottle on the desk in front of Marshal Bannon. He answered," This wine bottle has an extra bottom attached to it." Henry carefully removed the extra bottom. To their surprise, there was a small black pouch tucked inside of it. Henry gave the pouch to Marshal Bannon who carefully opened it. He gently emptied the pouch onto the desk. The small green gems came out of the pouch. Marshal Bannon asked," Henry where did you get this bottle?" Henry responded," I took it from the wagon behind Marcello's jewelry store. There was a wagon backed in behind the store. The crates were full of wine bottles." Marshal Bannon put the gems in the pouch. He replied," This bottle was stolen by you. I understand you wanted to show me, but I can't use it without implicating you. I am not going to arrest you for theft. I am going to investigate this further on my own within the limits of the law. I don't want you involved in any way. Do you understand?" Henry felt relieved he wasn't going to jail. He answered," I understand, and I promise I'll never do it again." Marshal Bannon put the pouch back inside the false bottom and then slip it on the bottle. He said," I'll give it to the jewelry store. I'll think up something." Marshal Bannon took the bottle to the jewelry store.

A young man was at the counter helping a customer. Marshal Bannon walked up to the counter. The young man noticed the bottle. After the customer left, he asked," May I help you, Marshal?" He answered," This bottle was turned into me. I am returning it to you because Marcello Winery owns this store, I am certain you'll return it to the winery." The young man took the bottle. He placed it on the desk by the corner. Not saying a word, Marshal Bannon left the store.

The morning train brought two Pinkerton Detectives to Roaring Springs. They walked off the train. They saw Agatha at her window. They approached her. The gentleman with neatly parted brown hair and trimmed mustache was dressed in a suit. The lady was dressed in a pantsuit had her chestnut hair pulled back in a bun behind her head. They were all business. They were here for a purpose. The gentleman asked," Could you direct me to the Sheriff or Marshal's office?" Agatha told them the Marshal's office was at the edge of town and the Sheriff's office across from it. They thank her as they walked away. They saw the Marshal coming out of the jewelry store. The gentleman loudly said," Pardon me, but would you be the Marshal?" The badge was visible on his shirt. Marshal Bannon turned his head to face them. He answered," I am Marshal Wil Bannon, may I help you?" The gentleman answered," Yes, we need to speak to you privately." He motioned for them to follow him to his office. After they walked into his office, they show them their credentials. He looked at their identifications. He was a little surprised Pinkerton Detectives came to town. The gentleman said," I am Detective Terence Scott, and this is my partner, Kara Trent. We are from New York." Kara responded," We were hired to retrieve stolen gems from a jeweler in New York. These gems are worth thousands of dollars raw, however, if cut, the gems double in price. We received a tip the gems are here." Suddenly Marshal Bannon had this funny feeling he may have seen those gems in the wine bottle. He carefully asked," Do have any further leads?" She answered," We would like to check out the jewelry store. It specializes in the rare gems." Detective Scott responded," If we find something interesting, we'll let you. Now, could you lead us in the direction of a place to stay?" Marshal Bannon answered," There is a hotel across the street and bed and breakfast at the far end of town, named Ma's Boarding House. Both places are reasonable and have good food. If you need to rent a rig, the liberty is by the train station." He watched them walk across the street to Roaring Springs Hotel.

Federico arrived at the jewelry store with his assistant, Gin Bo, and mother, Francesca. She noticed the bottle on the desk.

She asked," How did this bottle get on the desk? It should be on its way to South Bend." The young man replied," Marshal Bannon brought it in this morning. He stated the bottle was turned into him." Federico looked over the bottle. He noticed the clear seal going around it was broken. He carefully removed the bottom. He took the small sack out. He opened it to check for the emeralds. The stones were still inside. He said," The stones are still here, but the seal is broken. I'll check this next shipment myself. I'll hire two drivers to deliver to Pine Bluff tomorrow. This bottle will go with the next shipment. I'll tell the buyer there was a mix-up and reassure it won't happen again." Francesca responded," We'll ship directly from the winery until the person who removed the bottle is found. I don't want any problems especially the law getting wind of what we are doing. Now put the bottle in a safe place out of sight and increase the guards." Federico unlocked the storage room door of the wine bottles to place the bottle with the others. After he locked the door, he decided to walk to the stage office. It occurred to him to hire the stage driver because he would know the route the best.

Federico arrived at the stagecoach office. He saw Cassey and Georgia looking over the team of horses before leaving. It was a matter of time before their jobs come to an end. The train was taking their place. Cassey saw Federico standing by the office door looking at him. Cassey asks," Is there something I can help you with?" Smiling, Federico answered," Yes, I would like to hire both of you for a special delivery run. I'll pay both of you $500.00 each." Cassey and Georgia looked at him in disbelief. Georgia asked," What are we delivering for that kind of money?" Federico answered," A shipment of my best wine to the train station in Pine Bluff. The contact person is Kye Thorn. He'll be waiting for you."Cassey replied," We can do it tomorrow morning because we have a short day today. Is this acceptable with you?" Federico had hoped they leave right away, but the next day was fine too. Federico responded," Meet me at the winery tomorrow morning and I'll pay you before you leave." Cassey and Georgia watched Federico return to the jewelry store. Cassey saw Marshal Bannon walking up the street. Georgia hollered for him. When Marshal Bannon stopped in front of them, they told him about the job offer from Federico. He looked at them with a puzzled expression. They couldn't figure out why he would pay them a large sum of money to deliver wine. He said," Cassey, Georgia, pull the wagon over halfway there. I'll check the bottles for anything unusual." They agreed to meet at the crossroads by Pine Bluff tomorrow morning. Cassey and Georgia started their run.

Marshal Bannon continued walking to Silver Spur Saloon. He decided Henry should stay at the ranch until this was over. He had a strong feeling Henry may be in danger. He walked into the saloon looking for Henry. He asked," Sam, where is Henry?" Sam answered," Henry is in the storeroom washing glasses, Marshal." Sally went to get him. Henry came out with a tray of clean glasses. Marshal Bannon said," Henry, I need to talk to you." Henry sat the tray of glasses on the bar for Sam to put them away. He and Henry walked outside. Marshal Bannon checked his pocket watch. Charlie would be coming soon to town for the usual supply run for the ranch. Marshal Bannon said," My ranch hand's cook, Charlie needs help in the kitchen with cleanup and other odds and ends. You'll be paid a dollar a day plus keep." Henry responded," I accept and when can I start?" As Charlie came into town driving a buckboard, Marshal Bannon told him now. They met Charlie at the general store. Marshal Bannon said," Charlie, this is Henry. He'll be helping you from now on." Charlie and Henry shook hands. Charlie replied," It's about time. I've been after you and Cali for months to get me help. You can start by helping me get supplies." They walked into the general store.

Judge Thaddeus Ward arrived on the evening stage. His husky build stepped down from the stage. He had silver hair with a neatly trimmed beard. He wiped his wire-rim glasses with a handkerchief. Next, he brushed the dust off his blue suit with his hands. Cassey handed him his duffle bag. He walked to Marshal Bannon's office. When he walked in, Marshal Bannon was sitting at his desk. They greeted each other warmly. Judge Ward remembered swearing Marshal Bannon in when Marshal Westbrook became severely injured from pursuing cattle thieves. Marshal Bannon was the deputy then and caught the cattle thieves with the posse's help. Marshal Westbrook retired to his farm. Judge Ward sat down on the chair beside the desk. Marshal Bannon said," The surveyor and new Indian Agent will be arriving soon. The land in question was an old reservation. Tomas Marcello was the one who supposedly purchased the property. But another thing got my attention. I suspect Federico Marcello is in jewelry smuggling of rare gems. I received a tip about it. I promised I wouldn't reveal that person's name." Judge Ward thought for a moment before he replied," The land deed may be forged and the jewelry could be a part of this, too. This could be a very interesting case. Do we have any evidence thus far or is it speculation?" Marshal Bannon answered," Right now it is speculation until I gather more evidence. There are two Pinkerton Detectives in town looking for the stolen gems from New York. I only hope I get everything solved before they apprehend the person I am after."

Leaving out a sigh, Judge Ward said," I'll get a room at the hotel, and I'll be here until this is resolved within the boundaries of the law. Am I understood?" Marshal Bannon replied," I understand, Judge. Thank you for coming." Judge Ward stood up to leave. He gave a nod as he walked out the door.

Late in the evening, almost dusk, the burley driver for Marcello's Winery arrived at Federico's house. A quick knock on the door and the butler opened the door. He walked in carrying the empty whiskey bottle. Federico, Francesca, and Gin Bo were in the den discussing the possible routes they could alternate to deliver the special wine. They watched the burly driver walk into the den. They could tell by his facial expression he was somewhat upset. He gave the empty whiskey bottle to Francesca. Federico picked the whiskey bottle up. He looked at it as the driver said," This empty bottle was put in replace of the wine bottle in the crate. The buyer wasn't happy with the special wine bottle missing. I told him it won't happen again, and I'll redeliver a special case for him." Federico recalled seeing the town drunk near the wagon one night at the jewelry store. Gin Bo chased him away. Thoughts started swirling in his head about the town drunk returning and switching bottles. This would explain how the Marshal returned the wine bottle to the jewelry store because perhaps the town drunk figured out the wine bottle's bottom with the gems inside. The town drunk gave it to the Marshal. He put the whiskey bottle down on the desk. Bitterly he said," The whiskey bottle may have come from the town drunk. Gin Bo chased him away one night. I do believe he returned and did the switch." When the telephone rang, Francesca answered it. It was her brother-in-law, Tomas's brother, Luca, calling to tell her about the Pinkerton Detectives were on their trail about the gems. They only have speculation and to be cautious of any new buyers. Francesca thanked him as she hung up the telephone. She informed Federico and Gin Bo about the telephone call. Federico responded," We need to find the town drunk. I want to question him about the switch and if he found anything unusual about the wine bottle. The seal on the wine bottle was broken, but I'm not sure if he did it. We have a mess to clean up." Looking at the burly driver, Federico replied," We'll go to the jewelry store and remove all the wine from storage. You'll deliver it with my compliments to the buyer in South Bend and tell him everything is accounted for. We'll load the wagon for Pine Bluff in the morning from the winery. I'll send a special note with the bill for them to deliver to Kye Thorn. They'll never know what is really in the special folder.

This way if the Marshal or the Pinkerton's get nosy about the wine shipment, they'll never find the gems in the crates or the wine bottles bottom because the wine bottles used will have nothing extra, but wine only." Smiling, they left the house to go to the jewelry store in the freight wagon.

Henry was busy settling in with his new job. He helped Charlie make supper and clean up. He finally sat down on the bench outside to get a breath of fresh air. Charlie came outside carrying a jug and two cups. He said," I make my own Kentucky sippin mash. You'll have to drink it slowly, cause it'll set your head on fire, burn your inners, and make your kidneys scream. It can soothe the most savage beast, but it's sure is fine." He removed the cork from the jug. A small blue flame came from the opening. He poured a small amount in a cup for Henry. He gave it to Henry. Charlie poured some in his cup. Henry never tried this before. He slowly brought the cup to his lips. He did what Charlie told him. He took a small swallow of it. It was wickedly strong. He felt his eyes bug out. It was stronger than the whiskey he had drunk. Henry thought in a way it tasted a lot like apple cider with more spicy flavors as it went down Henry's throat. Smiling, Henry said," It sure is good." Charlie poured more in their cups. A friendship between them was forming. For the first time in a long time, they were no longer alone in the world. They spent the night enjoying the mash and cool night air. They told each other their life stories.

Casey and Georgia arrived at the Marcello Winery in the early morning. Federico and Gin Bo were waiting for them at the warehouse. They dismounted from their horses. The wagon was already loaded. Federico handed Casey the folder as he said," Give this to Kye Thorn when you deliver the wine. It is a bill for the shipment. You'll meet him at the train station." Federico paid Casey and Georgia $500.00 in cash. They climbed up into the freight wagon. Casey replied," We should return this afternoon." Gin Bo responded," There are riffles under your seat if you should run into trouble." Casey picked up the reins. Georgia laid a rifle across his lap. They were ready to go. Casey urged the six horses in a slow trot. The Marshal will be waiting for them at the crossroads, halfway point to Pine Bluff. The horses trotted down the dusty road. Georgia had his eyes searching for the Marshal. When he finally saw him by the trees on the long side of the road, he told Casey to stop the wagon by the trees. Marshal Bannon said," We need to check the bottles for anything unusual. For instance, an extra bottom or appearance of a seal going around the bottom." One by one the two crates were open.

The bottles were carefully looked over. All the bottles were the same. Casey replied," Doesn't look like anything unusual." The crates were closed back up. Casey and Georgia continued their way to Pine Bluff train station. Marshal Bannon proceed to town.

The surveyor Emmett Graff arrived. He stopped his wagon at the livery stable. His lanky build stepped down from the wagon. He removed his derby to wipe his brow. His thinning gray hair laid flat on his head. Quince saw the stranger walk toward him. The stranger stuck his hand out with a half-grin. He said," I am Emmett Graff, the surveyor. I need to board my horses and wagon." Shaking his hand, Quince responded," I am Quince, blacksmith. I'll put your horses up. The price is $2.00 a day, includes feed, water, and brushing. I'll put your wagon outback. The land office is down the street. You can't miss it." After Emmett paid him, he walked to the land office.

Harold was looking at the deeds. When Emmett walked in, he said," Good afternoon, Harold." Harold showed Emmett the papers as he asked," Emmett, could you figure out which property line is correct, and which is not?" Emmett looked at the maps and deeds. The two maps showed two different property lines. Emmett replied," I'll go out to Willow Creek in the morning. I'll compare the maps with my findings. I'll have an answer to your questions tomorrow." Judge Ward walked into the land office. After the introductions to each other, Harold gave the deeds to Judge Ward. He laid the two deeds on the counter. He looked over the deeds very carefully. Judge Ward picked up the one deed. He said," This deed is fake. I recognized the Indian Agent Adam Travis's name. I'll take this deed to Marshal Bannon. When you do the survey, try to make it accurate as possible. I'll need it for court. Harold, who surveyed the property before now? " Harold looked at the back of the map. He answered," Zac Jonas did the surveying for the county and the reservations. He did a few homesteads before he died from the fever that swept through the town hard." Emmett responded," I'll do the surveying tomorrow morning. I am not certain, but I think the property lines were moved." Judge Ward replied," I am at the hotel. When you are going to do the survey, let me know, I would like to be present." Emmett said," I'll be staying at Ma's Boarding House if you have any further questions." As Judge Ward walked out of the land office, he saw Marshal Bannon entering his office.

He still had the fake deed in his hand. He walked into the Marshal's office. He handed the fake deed to Marshal Bannon. Judge Ward said," This is the fake deed. Adam Travis altered the real deed by using this deed.

The real deed, he didn't know remained with the Willow Creek property. There is no bill of sale. Adam Travis gave the property to Tomas Marcello illegally. The land office did the paperwork under the disguise it was legal, but it wasn't. They were as wrong as Adam Travis and even worse Tomas Marcello received property he shouldn't have." Marshal Bannon replied," Harold, didn't run the land office ten years ago. Eric Baylor had the office. He left the town shortly after Tomas Marcello died from the fever. He could be anywhere by now." Judge Ward responded," I met the surveyor at the land office. His name is Emmett Graff. He'll be doing the surveying tomorrow. I told him I want to be present when he does it. I suspect you'll want to be there, too." Marshal Bannon said," I'll be there, but first I have to speak to Wise Owl, the Cherokee Shaman. I don't want any trouble from the living or the spirits. I must warn you there are stories about the property being haunted. You may see things that'll make you think twice before believing. Your eyes will not be deceiving in the things you may see. Just prepare yourself for anything unusual. Wise Owl will be helping us." Judge Ward looked at Marshal Bannon for a moment. Being he was lost for words, he told him he'll see him tomorrow. Marshal Bannon decided to go see Wise Owl for him to be ready for the next day.

CHAPTER 04

There is always work to be done on the ranch, but occasionally I would go for a ride to relax. It was a glorious day for a pleasure ride. The sun was shining. The air was cool and crisp. A perfect Spring Day to take a break from work. I urged my horse into a slow trot down by the creek. When I saw my pa coming down the road, I rode up to him. We stopped our horses. Shortly thereafter Running Fawn rode her horse up to us. I said," Hi, pa. I thought I take a break and enjoy this Spring Day." He replied," I am glad I ran into both of you. I want both of you here tomorrow morning for the surveying. I'm going to talk to Wise Owl to help us with spirits if they chose to show up. Judge Ward will be here and Dottie, too." Running Fawn responded," It is good the truth is finally being told. The spirits will be pleased. You'll find Wise Owl with Little Eagle. Yellow Feather gave him a son. It is a happy day for them." As he started riding toward the reservation, he said," I'll congratulate them both, thank you for telling me." Looking at Running Fawn, I asked," Do you want to join me for a ride?" Smiling, she answered," I will be happy to join you." We urged our horses into a slow trot down past the creek.

When we came upon a small waterfall, we stopped to give the horses a break. We dismounted by the trees. I could tell there was something on Running Fawn's mind. She seemed to be lost in her thoughts. She sat down on a rock staring into the water. She was looking for answers to her questions. I sat down beside her. I asked," Something on your mind?" She answered," I saw Peat once picking blackberries, second time getting fish traps. He stirs something in me when we look into each other's eyes. His hands were soft and gentle when he touched mine. Is it wrong for me to fall in love with a simple look and touch?" I answered," You're not wrong. Sometimes that's all it takes. There is a connection you felt with him." Smiling, she replied," The feeling makes me happy." Pausing for a moment, a look of sadness came upon her face. She sadly said," My world will not accept him, and his world will not accept me." She was told stories about the white men taking Indian maidens as wives, but never being accepted in their world. The Indian maidens were called squaw among other names. They were looked down upon. They were sometimes humiliated and abused as were the children if they had any to the white man. She brought her thoughts on the special event of Yellow Flowers and Little Eagle's baby. Their parents and the whole village will celebrate the birth. From the waterfall, we rode to the village to join the celebration.

It seemed to brighten Running Fawn's mood. I saw my parents there. Wise Owl asked us to help him make the sacred hoop in the morning and we agreed.

Dawn came with Wise Owl, Running Fawn and I collecting the stones to make a circle on sacred ground. A stone circle was finally formed. A fire ring in the middle with special stones. He picked the herbs needed for the tea. The wood gathered for the fire was placed in the circle. Next, we created places to sit with the fur blankets. He started the fire. Using a feather, he waved the smoke over him as he did a chanting prayer. He was asking the Great Spirit for a good day to see the truth.

Marshal Bannon went to the newspaper office. Dottie was busy setting print when he walked in. He quickly told her about the surveying. She grabbed her tablet and pencil. Emmett was coming up the street in his wagon. Judge Ward walked over to them. Emmett stopped his wagon in front of them. Marshal Bannon said," I presume you're the surveyor." Emmett replied," I am, and I am going there now if you lead the way." Marshal Bannon responded," This is Dottie, newspaper editor and Judge Ward you already know. You follow my horse and I'll lead there. Dottie and Judge Ward will follow in their rig." Dottie said," Judge Ward you can ride in my rig. I'll go get it from the livery stable." She walked down to the livery stable. Marshal Bannon mounted his horse. In a few minutes, she came up the street driving her rig. She stopped her rig in front of Judge Ward. Once he was seated, everyone followed Marshal Bannon to Willow Creek.

Wise Owl greeted them as they rode up to him. Marshal Bannon did the introductions for Judge Ward and Emmett. They followed Wise Owl to the stone circle. Wise Owl said," Step inside the sacred hoop. Sit by the fire." Once everyone was seated, Wise Owl gave us cups for the tea. He said," Drink the tea. The tea will keep you calm during the journey." We were nervous and a little scared of what was going to happen next. When we took a drink of tea, it seemed to soothe our nerves and gave a calming effect. We were quiet. Wise Owl used a large wooden spoon to pour water on the rocks, creating smoke. He replied," It is to clear the air for the spirits to come." Emmett softly said," Father help us." Wise Owl looked at him. He responded," Do not be afraid. The sacred hoop will protect you. The spirits will not harm you." Pausing for a moment to put more water on the rocks. Looking up to the sky, Wise Owl said, " Great Spirit, come, show us the truth through your eyes." The wind started to blow. The leaves in the trees were rustling. The water in the creek started rippling louder. We started seeing the past.

The village is bustling with life. Children playing and laughing. Women taking care of the fresh game. The men getting ready for the next hunt. It was a peaceful scene. Then things started to turn for the worse. On the bridge was the Indian Agent, Adam Travis meeting three other men. They greeted each other by their names, Tomas, Zac, and Eric. Tomas wearing a dark suit with black hair removed an envelope from his inside jacket pocket. He paid Adam, Zac, and Eric money. Eric wearing a brown suit, bald, gave Tomas papers in a folder. Adam standing there in a gray suit, said," Now you have the land, and no questions asked. I'm glad to get rid of them. I found some men to run them off. If they capture the women, I can sell them along the border." Zac had a scruffy appearance as he counted the money said," Thanks, it was good doing business with you." He was the first to leave. Eric followed, after shoving the money in his suit jacket.

Suddenly riders came out of nowhere to meet Adam and Tomas at the tree line along the road. They were roughing-looking men, about a dozen or more. Tomas approached a nasty-looking man sitting on a black horse. Tomas gave him an envelope. The nasty man removed the money to count it. Snarling he said," It's all here. Me and my boys are going to have some fun." They galloped their horses into the village, shooting everything in sight. Adam and Tomas rode away. Women and children were screaming. The men trying their best to defend them. They let out war cries. There was chaos everywhere. Emily grabbed her son as she ran toward the creek. She slipped and fell, down over the embankment. Strong Bear was shot going to her. Someone picked her up and put her on a buckboard. Her son was picked up by the same person. Both were unconscious as the person took them away on the buckboard. Approaching riders scared them away. It was the Marshal and Sheriff.

When the wind stopped, we were in the present. We stood up looking at each other. The truth was ugly. Judge Ward said," If I didn't see it with my own eyes, I would never have believed it. Those who are guilty are dead or whereabouts unknown. It is shameful." Emmett was still rattled by it. Shaking he replied," I'll a... get started on the... surveying." Marshal Bannon helped him stand up. The face of the nasty man stayed in my mind. I saw his face somewhere. I closed my eyes, and it came to me. He was older, but I was certain it was Dirty Birch. I jumped to my feet. I said," I recognized the nasty man. I'm pretty sure it was Dirty Birch." Marshal Bannon responded," I agree. One question, how do we find him?" I answered," Smokin Peat may have an idea where we can find him. I think I know where I can find Smokin Peat. Running Fawn, are you with me?" She answered," Lead the way, I'll be with you." Dottie was writing about what she saw. She had to word it carefully. Some would think they were imagining things. Emmett became lost in his thoughts with surveying the land. Deputy Barixa came riding toward us. Marshal Bannon approached his horse. Deputy Barixa said," You need to come to town. The new Indian Agent arrived. He has a surprise for you." Marshal Bannon told Emmett he'll be back. He rode off with Deputy Barixa. Dottie and Judge Ward decided to stay to watch Emmett work.

Running Fawn and I proceeded to our horses. We started the search for Smokin Peat. I knew he had to be around somewhere. Running Fawn suggested looking by the blackberry bushes where she first saw him. We came upon a grove. Among the trees, Smokin Peat was there. He was surprised to see us. We rode up to each other. We exchanged hellos. Smokin Peat happily asked," What are you doing here?" I answered," We need your help to find Dirty Birch Sayer. I thought you might know where he is." Smokin Peat had to think about it. Running Fawn responded," He is the one who raided my village. He killed many of my people. Please help us find him."

Smokin Peat replied," I think I know, but let me take care of it. I don't want you hurt. Once I find him, I'll let your pa know. He is a bad man." Running Fawn and Smokin Peat looked at each other before riding off. One could see they had feelings for each other.

Joseph Silver came with Elly Strong and her son, Berry Strong. Marshal Bannon met them at his office. Joseph Silver average build wearing a blue suit, had black hair stood by the window of the office. Elly shook Marshal Bannon's hand as did her son and Joseph. Elly said," I was the teacher on the Cherokee reservation. My husband was Strong Bear. He was killed during the raid." Marshal Bannon asked," Who took you and your son away?" Joseph answered," I did. I was a new Indian Agent in training. Adam Travis was training me. I was horrified by what I saw happening. I saw Elly falling and her son injured, I had to do something. I took them far away. My wife and I changed their clothes before the doctor saw them. I knew if they look Indian, they wouldn't get treated. The doctor was told it was a buggy accident. When they got better, Elly took her son to Maine. I gave them money for the train tickets. I reported the incident to my superiors, but they did nothing." Elly replied," I took my son to my sister in Maine. Being he looked like me, it was easier to live our lives quietly. Unfortunately, my son had to deny a part of his life, to live unharmed. I explained to him the best I could. He was bitter about it for quite some time. Eventually, he overcame it by the love of my brother-in-law, his uncle and aunt and I helped him. His cousins accepted him and that helped. They only knew his father was killed in an outlaw raid on our farm, but never told him he was Cherokee. I renamed my son Berry. A part of his name, Little Bear. I took the last name Strong to honor my husband.

I put the gold band on my finger to honor our marriage, even though it is not recognized by the white man." Berry responded," Marshal, I saw the man who killed my father. I told my mother I want justice for my father. I was nine years old, but I still remember as if it happened yesterday. My father was coming toward us when he was shot. I screamed. My mother fell, down over a bank holding my hand. From there I don't remember. I woke up and a doctor looking at me." Marshal Bannon reached for a wanted poster of Dirty Birch Sayer picture on it. He gave it to Berry. The picture showed a good drawing of the face of Dirty Birch Sayer. Berry confirmed it was him. Marshal Bannon said," The land is being surveyed. Judge Ward is here and told everything. I know I can't undo the hurt and tragic loss of your father, but I am going to see justice is done." Joseph replied," We'll get a room at Ma's Boarding House. The stage driver recommended the place. I would like to go to the reservation once we have our rooms." Marshal Bannon offered to escort them to Ma's Boarding House.

The two Pinkerton Detectives were observing the Marcello Jewelry store from Pearl's Café. The outside dining area was open to the public from being closed during the winter months. They ate their lunch of potatoes, ham, biscuits, and coffee. They noticed Francesca, Federico, and Gin Bo arriving in their carriage, stopping at the jewelry store. A few minutes later the carriage left with Federico and Gin Bo. Francesca walked into the jewelry store. The carriage stopped again at an office building. Federico and Gin Bo stepped out of the carriage. They were going to see their attorney about the property they wanted to buy. Kara noticed how Federico walked into the door of the building. This gave her an idea. Kara said," I think I know how to get Federico talking." Terence asked," What are your ideas?" She answered," Federico walks with arrogance and pride and that will be his downfall. You pretend to be my brother and here to buy wine for a restaurant. I'll be the sister interested in rare jewelry. I'll be the lady that will have him wrapped around her little finger." Terence replied," He may be hard to break. He might be suspicious of us, because of being new customers he might not want to do business with us. We could be dealing with an employee instead. It could make breaking the case harder." Kara responded," Never underestimate the power of a lady. Trust me, it'll work." Terence replied," We should inform the Marshal and the office about our plan. If something goes wrong, the Marshal would be the only one that could help save us." After they finished eating, they walked to the Marshal's office.

Marshal Bannon had returned to his office from Ma's Boarding House. He was getting ready to go to the reservation when Terence and Kara walked up to him. They quickly told him about their plan. Marshal Bannon said," I want to let you know Judge Ward is here. The Marcello's is being investigated for land fraud. We work together, we can get everything solved. You keep me informed on what's going on and I'll help you to get your case solved." Terence replied," Actually, being we will be undercover, you'll need to pretend to arrest us with him. Once he is behind bars, we will reveal who we are. Is this acceptable, Marshal?" Nodding in agreement, Marshal Bannon responded," It would be best. Now if you excuse me, I have somewhere to be. But keep me posted." They told him they will as they left the office to prepare to capture Federico.

Marshal Bannon rode with the Indian Agent, Joseph Silver, Elly, and Berry to the reservation. Morning Star was carrying a basket of corn when she saw them. It may have been ten years since she saw them, but she remembered the flaming hair. A smile came to her face as she shouted," Elly, is it you?" Joseph stopped the buggy for Elly to greet Morning Star with a hug. Berry stepped down from the buggy. Marshal Bannon stopped his horse. Chief Eagle approached them. It took him a few minutes to recognize them. A smile came across his copper face. He said," Honey Bear, Little Bear you have come home." Happily, Elly replied," I am glad to be finally home. Little Bear has grown up. He is a fine young man. Strong Bear would be pleased." Berry hesitated at first. Finally shaking

Chief Eagle's hand, he said," It is good to be home. I thought I would never see you again." Marshal Bannon responded," Forgive me for interrupting your happy reunion. Chief Eagle, I would like for you to meet the new Indian Agent Joseph Silver." Chief Eagle noticed Joseph's dark hair and eyes. He asked," Are you half?" Joseph answered," I am part Cherokee. My father is Cherokee, and my mother is white. She chose to be with my father. She was a minister's daughter who came with him to the reservation to teach their religious beliefs. Soon they learn the Cherokee is as spiritual as them. My parents are still there." Pausing for a moment to look around the reservation, he continued speaking," Chief Eagle, we should talk about relocating to Oklahoma. The Cherokee reservation is there. Most of the Cherokee have been relocated there. I'll be the one in charge of it." Chief Eagle replied," Before I speak to you about Oklahoma, I have something to do first. Little Bear, come with me." Chief Eagle walked to a corral of horses. Berry followed behind him. He watched Chief Eagel open the gate. Next, Chief Eagle led a horse to Berry. The horse was dark brown with a white blaze on the face. Chief Eagle gave the lead rope to Berry.

He said," Little Bear, this was your Adadoda's horse. I think you should have him. I have the hunting knife, bow, and arrows your Adadoda used. I saved them for you." Emily walked up to them with Morning Star. They were overwhelmed with emotions. They were happy and yet sad. Berry softly replied," I thank you. This the best gift I could ever receive." He gave the horse a few pats on the neck. Morning Star responded," Elly, Berry, there has been someone waiting for you. Go to the Wahkan Gadohi, you'll see him." Elly and Berry walked across the bridge. Running Fawn and I returned to the reservation. We watched from the distance as Strong Bear appeared before Elly and Berry. Everyone stopped what they were doing to watch the reunion between them unfold.

Strong Bear saw Elly and Berry. He dismounted from his horse. Suddenly the word for father in Cherokee came to Berry. Smiling he said," Adadoda." They were scared. The happiness of seeing him erased their fears. Tears of joy streamed down their faces. It has been ten long painful years of waiting to see him once more. They thought this day would never come. Now they can finally have peace in their hearts. Strong Bear gently said," Cubby, you remembered me. Honey Bear, it does my heart good to see you both. Now, you both live for me. My love will always be you." He gently caressed her face. They kissed one last time. Strong Bear hugged his son. Berry could feel his strong arms around him. Berry softly whispered," See you, again, Adadoda". A soft breeze surrounded them. Someday they would see each other again until then they would keep each other in their hearts. They watched Strong Bear drift away in the breeze. He was finally at peace. A soft voice in the breeze said," Good-bye, my love." Elly and Berry hugged each other. They were able to move on. They walked up to Morning Star and Chief Eagle feeling peaceful at last.

Marshal Bannon rode over to Judge Ward who was assisting Emmett with the surveying. They were still in disbelief at what they saw. The land in their strong opinion was indeed haunted, however, they knew no one would believe them. Dottie was lost for words. She had to be creative in writing this story without people questioning her insanity. She walked around the property. Often, she would stop to write something down on her tablet. Marshal Bannon asked, "How is everything going?" Judge Ward answered," We're almost done. Is there something you would like to tell me?" Marshal Bannon informed him about Pinkerton's plan to capture Federico Marcello and Indian Agent talking to Chief Eagle. He proceeds to tell him about Elly and her son. Judge Ward replied," The land will be reverted to you. This was originally a part of your family's ranch.

Your father gave this land to Indian Affairs with an agreement it is returned if they were to leave by their own free will. I did some research before coming here. I had a feeling when you said about the land dispute, this was it." Marshal Bannon responded," Chief Eagle and his people are good friends with my family. When my father first started this ranch, it was rough. Chief Eagle's father, Chief Red Bird saved us from nearly starvation. A blizzard came and we were running out of food. My pa went hunting for food. Chief Red Bird and his warriors found my pa by the creek half frozen to death. They brought him to the house with a deer. My ma and I were grateful to him. We nursed pa back to health. From then on, a friendship formed. Chief Eagle and I grew up together. I do my best to ensure they live in peace. A greedy man threatens their existence. I can't allow that." Emmett started gathering his equipment up. He placed everything in his wagon. He took his notes to Judge Ward and Marshal Bannon. Emmett said," I have two corner stakes in place. I'll have it finished by tomorrow. I want to review the map again. The property is 540 acres." They weren't expecting that much land to be incorrectly surveyed. Dottie, Judge Ward, and Emmett drove to town. Marshal Bannon walked up to Wise Owl. He told him they would return the next day.

At the reservation, Morning Star, Elly, and Running Star started to prepare dinner. Joseph and Chief Eagle continue their talk about relocating in his house made of woven saplings, plastered with mud and roofed with poplar bark. Joseph told Chief Eagle about the Oklahoma reservation more entailed. Chief Eagle sat and listened intently. He wanted a place for his people to feel safe. This place thus far has been safe with the exceptions of a few white men harassing them in town and a few hunts. Marshal Bannon and Sheriff Micca always maintain peace for them. They would be among their people. He would discuss it with Wise Owl. Running Fawn overheard the conversation. She heard questions being asked and answered about the trip. She looked at her mother. They finished eating in silence. They were lost in their thoughts. Emily and Berry offered to help Morning Star to clean up. The evening sun was slowly setting. Joseph bid Chief Eagle a good night. Elly and Berry gave their goodbyes. Berry decided to ride his father's horse to the boarding house. My pa and I escorted Joseph, Elly, and Berry to Ma's Boarding House. We were glad to go home.

The naming ceremony of Little Eagle and Yellow Flower's baby came on the fourth day of their son's birth with blue skies and plenty of sunshine. It was as though the Great Spirit was happy for them. My ma and I went ahead of my pa to the reservation. He went to get Joseph, Elly, and Berry for the special day. Dottie saw them leaving town and she decided to come to the special event. Running Fawn and I started helping Morning Star to get ready by gathering wood by the creek. A prayer circle was formed by stone. A fire ring in the middle. When Dottie arrived, she became fascinated by the event. I saw her looking around. She was writing notes on the pad. I approached her. Smiling, she asked," Cali, could you explain what is happening here" I answered," Come with me I'll introduce you to Wise Owl's wife, Kachina Tiva, in English, Spirit Dancer. She is a Shaman too. She'll be performing the ceremony." Intrigued Dottie followed me to their house. Spirit Dancer was preparing for the ceremony. I introduce Spirit Dancer to Dottie. Dottie asked," Could you explain to me about the ceremony? I have never seen anything like it." Spirit Dancer smiled at her. She answered," It is a naming ceremony. The choosing of the name for the baby is given. I wave the baby over a fire four times while I say a prayer. The baby is then dipped in water seven times. Four Guides are chosen and are given herbs as gifts. The name is not stuck for all life. The name can be changed later in life to reflect the personality and acts of accomplishments, great or small." Dottie replied," The English way is you're stuck with a name until death." Spirit Dancer responded," A person changes with time, good or bad. It is, for this reason, we believe the name should be the reflection of the person within." Morning Star came to tell us everything was ready to begin.

Spirit Dancer stood in the middle of the circle. Little Eagle and Yellow Flower brought their son into the circle. Spirit Dancer asked," Did you choose the four guides?" Little Eagle answered," Yes, we chose Doc Sherry and Wil Bannon. Clever Fox and his wife, Graceful Doe." Spirit Dancer replied," The four guides come forward, join us in the sacred circle." I watched my parents walk into the circle smiling. They were happy to be chosen. Clever Fox and Graceful Doe stood by my parents. Spirit Dancer asked," Little Eagle, Yellow Flower, why have you chosen these four guides?" Yellow Flower answered," Doc Sherry helped our son come to this life. Marshal Bannon is an honest lawman. Clever Fox and Graceful Doe will help our son become the man he is destined to be by teaching him friendship." Spirit Dancer replied," Let us begin. Place your son in my arms." Yellow Flower placed their son in Spirit Dancer's arms. The beautiful baby boy cooed in his blanket as Spirit Dancer removed the blanket from him. After she gave the blanket to Yellow Flower, she started to wave the baby over the fire. Spirit Dancer said," Great Spirit, I hear the whose voice in the wind. The breath of life for all the living. I come before you. Two of dust and bones created one. May Mother Earth provide the seasons to grow and be strong. May Father Sky wrap around you clear skies with Grandfather Sun to brighten your days.

May Grandmother Moon, light your journeys at night and the stars as your guide. We honor fire by asking to keep you warm on cold nights and your heart glowing with love. We honor Wind for you to sail calmly through life's journeys. We honor Water for you to be clean and your thirst for knowledge is quenched. Great Spirit with all you created may this child grow in harmony, peace, and happiness. Aho" Next, Spirit Dancer dipped the baby in the water seven times. Once she was done, she placed him in the blanket. She responded," Emoli, is now ready to begin his journey. Four guides you will be responsible for guiding him on his life's journey. Now let's celebrate the beginning of his life." Dottie whispered to me," What does Emoli mean?" I softly answered," It means Black Fox." The music started to play, songs were being sung, dancing around the fire, and eating good food started. It was a day filled with joy.

CHAPTER 05

At the hotel in town, the Pinkerton Detective Kara Trent unpacked her dress from the trunk she brought with her. She laid the dress on the bed. She removed a jewelry box filled with antique necklaces, earrings, bracelets, and rings. Her grandmother's jewelry always went with her dresses. She placed the jewelry box on the dresser. A makeup pouch was placed on the dresser next to the jewel box. Terence knocked on the door. She opened it. When he walked in, he asked," what name shall we use for this ruse?" She thought about it for a minute. After she sat down on the chair, she answered," Noah and Arabella Canton of New York." He sat down on the bench next to the chair. He replied," For this to work we need to check out of here and check-in somewhere else under those names. I think he'll check us out. If we are here under our real names, it could be a disaster." She responded," Good idea. You check us out while I put on my dress. I'll slip out the back door. We can meet at Ma's Boarding House." He started gathering her bags. He placed the trunk and satchel out in the hall to be taken downstairs when she was finished. He returned to his room to pack his bags and alter his appearance. He put on glasses, a fake beard with long sideburns, and a derby hat. She proceeded to change into her blue Victorian dress. She applied light makeup on. Lastly, she placed her grandmother's antique brass and ruby necklace with matching earrings on. She let her chestnut hair flow down over her shoulders. She placed a barrette to pull her sides up. She picked up her reticule to put her hankie, some money, and 2 shot derringer for protection. She placed everything in the trunk. Terence started carrying the trunk downstairs. She picked up the satchel. While Terence kept the front desk clerk busy with signing out, she carefully slipped out the back door to the waiting buggy. Terence thought about arriving by buggy at Ma's Boarding House would look better. Lucky for him the livery stable had one available.

Ma's Boarding House was a large eight-bedroom house run by an older widow. Her children grew and moved away. Her husband passed during the fever epidemic. She included three square meals in the price. A washroom for the guests was off the laundry room adjacent to the kitchen. A wrap-around porch with a hanging swing and benches greeted guests. Ma had her gray hair in a bun with an apron around her waist. She always greeted her guests with a smile. Another woman named Bonnie helped her. Somedays they were busier than others. Bonnie stopped sweeping the porch when she heard the buggy approaching. Terence stopped the buggy by the steps.

She looked at the gentleman in the suit. Terence asked," Do you have room for two more guests?" Smiling, she answered," Yes, we have room for two more. Welcome to Ma's Boarding House, I am Bonnie. Ma is in the kitchen." Ma heard the chatter from the kitchen window. She stepped outside to greet them. Bonnie said," May, we have two more guests." May replied," Welcome, I am May, the owner. The rate is $2.50 a week for each guest includes three meals a day. Everyone eats in the dining room. There is a washroom for you to freshen up. Towels and washcloths are on the shelves by the washbasin. If you agree, Bonnie can show you your rooms once you register." Kara and Terence stepped out of the buggy. Bonnie looked at Kara. She never saw a lady dress so fancy. Seeing a gentleman in a suit was something she was accustomed to seeing. They walked up the steps onto the porch. He responded," This is my sister, Arabella and I am her brother Noah Canton from New York. We are here on business. We do accept your terms and rates." After they signed the register book, they followed Bonnie up the stairs to their rooms. Terence retrieved their baggage and trunk from the buggy. Kara unpacked her jewelry and makeup, placed them on the dresser. Her work clothes remained packed in the closet. Her dresses were unpacked and neatly hung in the closet. A quick two knock on the door was a signal from Terence. It was time to go to Marcello's winery.

They ambled down the steps. May told them supper would be at six. Terence asked," May, could you direct us to the Marcello Winery?" May answered," It's easy to find. Follow the road to the outskirts of town about half a mile and it's on the left. There's a large sign at the road entrance." Kara responded," Thank you and we'll see you at six." Kara and Terence proceeded to walk out the door. Kara wrapped her lace-fringed shawl around her. Terence helped her into the buggy. Once he was seated, he picked up the reins. He urged the team of horses to go a slow trot.

When they arrived at Marcello Winery, they stopped at the shop. They walked into the shop. They noticed the wine glasses and various goblets. The rows of various wine bottles had their sections. A tasting area of tables and chairs was at the far end of the shop with a bay window view of the vineyard. Crackers and cheese were on the tables. Federico stopped talking to his employees when he saw her walk in. He quickly straightens his tie. He watched her looking at the red goblets. He hadn't seen a lady dress with such elegance around here. He looked at her ivory skin, lips of roses, long flowing chestnut hair carefully kept back with a diamond barrette, and soft teddy bear eyes when she glanced at him.

The ruby and brass necklace were placed across her cleavage perfectly. He was mesmerized by her appearance. He slowly walked up to her. The smell of her lilac perfume made him smile. As he did a partial bow, he took her hand to kiss it. Smiling, he said," Please allow me to introduce myself. I am Federico Marcello, owner of this winery. How may I help you?" Kara purposely, gently laid her hand on Federico's chest. She could feel his heart beating like a bass drum. She looked into his dark eyes. She noticed his coal-black hair was combed back and off the collar. She saw he had chiseled features. His thin red lips formed a sheepish smile, revealing pearly white teeth. His heart was captured. She softly said," I am Arabella Canton and my brother, Noah." Gin Bo saw the interaction between them. He thought her actions were suspicious. He would watch her carefully. Terence and Federico shooked hands. Terence said," I am here to purchase wine for the Candlelight Restaurant in New York." Federico replied," I can take your order, but first allow me the privilege to talk to your sister over dinner." Federico and Kara gazed into each other's eyes. Kara responded," My brother and I already have dinner plans. Perhaps we could have lunch tomorrow and you could give me a personal tour of your winery." The idea thrilled Federico. Happily, he replied," I look forward to it. Where are you staying?" She softly answered," Ma's Boarding House, room 7. I shall see you tomorrow." She gave him a quick peck on the cheek before they left. Noah and Federico agreed to do the order the next day. Gin Bo wrote down the Candle Light Restaurant's name. Federico walked her out to their buggy. Terence and Kara bid goodbye to Federico.

Gin Bo decided to telephone the Candlelight Restaurant to verify their information. To his surprise, the manager verified Noah Canton had permission to purchase wine for the restaurant. He told Federico their information was correct. He still had his doubts. Something didn't feel right to him.

During supper at Ma's Boarding House, the telephone rang. Agatha answered the telephone. It was for Noah Canton. Terence walked up to the telephone. The caller on the other end informed him in code that the road ahead was cleared and proceed with caution. He hung up the telephone, smiling. The Candlelight Restaurant's owner was a good client of the Pinkerton Detective Agency and often provided coverage for various cases. Terence sat down at the dining room table to finish eating his supper. Kara looked at him. He leaned toward her to whisper," We're in." They finished eating in silence. She was thinking to herself her plan was working. The tricky part was coming, to get information without blowing their cover.

In the morning, Judge Ward met marshal Bannon at his office. Sheriff Micca escorted Francesca and Federico Marcello to Marshal Bannon's office. Federico sent Gin Bo to have their attorney present. Christina Lauren walked into Marshal Bannon's office with Gin Bo following behind her. Deputy Barixa escorted Indian Agent, Joseph Silver, Elly, and Berry to his office. Once everyone was present, Judge Ward said," I Am Judge Ward and here today because injustice has occurred. At the request of Marshal Bannon, an investigation started about possible land fraud. He requested my presence to ensure the laws on this matter were legal and correct. Mrs. Marcello, the property your husband purchased before his death by Willow Creek will be reverted to Diamon Rose Ranch. The deed was falsified by the land office clerk who worked there at that time. The previous surveyor altered the property lines to make the property appear to have more than it was in actual size. Being you were not present during the transaction, you will not be charged for land fraud." Judge Ward gave the actual deed and altered deed to their attorney to be examined. Christina looked over the papers. Next, she showed the deeds to Francesca. Both knew they had to accept the loss of the property. They did not legally own it. Federico walked in disgust. Gin Bo followed behind him. Elly took this opportunity to voice her feelings to Tomas Marcello's widow. Elly felt she should be told about the pain Tomas caused her. Elly said," Mrs. Marcello, I know you don't know me, but I am Elly Strong and this is my son, Berry. Your husband, Tomas wanted me to leave my husband. His name was Strong Bear, a Cherokee Warrior. Strong Bear was a loving husband and father. Tomas became angry when I refused him. I could not get him to understand Strong Bear and I loved each other very much. I know my marriage to Strong Bear wasn't legal by our laws, but I consider him to be my husband. We were married by the Cherokee ceremony. Tomas sent men to force everyone off the land. My husband was killed protecting me and our son. I blame your husband, who was greedy, selfish, and cruel to others." Francesa stood there in shock for a few minutes. She had to think about all that transpired. She let out a sigh. It took a stranger to open her eyes to what she already knew about her husband. She replied," Mrs. Strong, I am sorry for the loss of your husband. My marriage to Tomas was arranged by our parents. There was no love in our marriage. Once our son was born, it was the last time Tomas and I was together. Tomas felt he did his duty by creating an heir. He was not a good man. Our son was sent to boarding school because Tomas didn't like being a father. I am envious of you. You were fortunate to have a husband who wanted to be a husband and loved you and your son."

Francesca looked at Elly with sadness in her eyes. Christina returned the papers to Judge Ward as she said," We will conduct business as usual on the property Mrs. Marcello owns legally." They quietly left the office. Elly said," Marshal Bannon, we will be leaving today. We will be returning to Main. Berry will be taking his horse with us. The train has a livestock car we will be using. We better get going the train will be leaving soon. One more thing, we thank both of you for helping to bring peace to our lives." After shaking their hands, Joseph escorted them to the train station.

Francesca returned to her house. She saw Federico standing in the den. She said," Federico, we need to talk." He replied," I know Father wasn't a good man. He didn't love us. He never did. I remember when I was a boy, I went to him to show him my report card. I was excited because I had all A's. I was certain Father would be pleased to see it, but I was wrong. Father told me he was a busy man and didn't have time for trivial matters. I quickly soon realize he was not interested in me or anything I did. Fortunately, I had you, my nanny, and school. Mother, I know you did your best. Why did you stay married to him?" Francesca walked up to the bay window in the den. Gazing out the window, she answered," Divorce is forbidden in Catholic marriages. Our marriage was arranged by our parents. Toms's family was in the winery business and my family was in the jewelry business. Our parents did business together. They thought it would be a good idea for their children to marry. The two businesses would become one. Our parents wanted a grandchild. They relish being your grandparents. Tomas and I never grew to love each other. He was a hard and bitter man. We considered each other to be business partners." She paused for a moment to look at Federico. She continued speaking," I have decided to return to New York permanently. I stopped living far too long. It is time I see my family. I have nieces and nephews I have yet to meet. You can sell out or continue to run the businesses without me, your decision." Federico asked," When are you leaving?" She answered," I'll take the afternoon train in Pine Bluff tomorrow. I'll pack a few things and then send for the rest when I get settled." He replied," I think I'll sell out. I like the idea of returning to New York permanently. I'll escort you to the train station tomorrow. I'll come to New york later. For now, I have a lunch date with a beautiful lady and her brother wants to buy wine for Candlelight Restaurant." She responded," Be cautious my son. You can't trust someone you don't know very well." Smiling, he said," I'll be careful. Once I clear the deal on the wine order,

Francesca walked upstairs to her bedroom. She started packing a few of her things in a trunk and duffle bags. Federico went to the winery shop.

Terence and Kara arrived at the winery shop a few minutes early. Federico greeted them warmly at the entrance of the shop. Federico said," Being it's a beautiful day, I decided we should have lunch in the courtyard." He offered his arm to Kara. She intertwined her arm with his arm. Tilting her head slightly toward him, she softly smiled at him. They slowly walked to the courtyard. Terence observed the warehouse near the wine shop. The workers were busy loading crates of wine. After they sat down at the table, servants brought them their lunch. Kara sat beside Federico. She purposely did this to get his attention. She wanted him to relax around her, to let his guard down. Terence sat across from Federico. They were served wine with fried chicken, potatoes, and rolls. While they ate lunch, Terence and Federico discussed the wine order. Federico told him about the strawberry and watermelon wines. Terence told Federico he would take fifty cases of each. The order pleased Federico. Once they finished eating, Federico offered to do the tour. Secretly, Federico was hoping Terence would leave him and Kara alone. He wanted to give the personal tour by their selves. An idea came to him. Federico said," Noah if your too busy to do the tour, I can take Arabella to Ma's Boarding House after the tour is over, but if that is acceptable with Arabella." She replied," I accept your offer." Terence responded," I, too accept your offer. We can settle the bill later." Smiling, Federico said," Good, it is settled then. Arabella, shall we begin the tour?" She answered," Yes, show me everything and tell me all about it. I am interested." Terence excused himself. He was leaving as they began the tour by carriage ride of the vineyard. Federico gave her the grand tour. He showed her where the red wine bottles were made to the strawberry patches and watermelons grew. They walked through the wine storage building and the warehouse to show her the wine ready to be shipped were in crates. She would ask questions and he delightfully answered. They were enjoying each other's company. When the tour was over, he told the coachman to Ma's Boarding house. During the ride, Federico told Kara he selling everything to relocate to New York. This surprised her. She mentioned the jewelry store in town. He told her it would be sold too. She decided they would have to move fast to find the missing gems. After arriving at Ma's Boarding House, he helped her out of the carriage. He asked," May I kiss you good night?" She thought he meant on the cheek or her hand. She softly said," Yes, you may." He ever so gently took her in his arms and kissed her passionately on the lips.

She put her arms around him as she felt his sweet soft lips kiss her. When he released his arms from around her, he softly said," Good night, and I shall see you tomorrow." She stepped away from him. She replied," A good night to you too. We'll see you tomorrow." He stepped into the carriage feeling happy. She watched the carriage drive away.

Terence stepped outside to see her. They looked at each other for a moment. She said," I think I need a doctor. I feel slightly ill." Terence remembered seeing the doctor's office by the café. He quickly retrieved the buggy from the stable. They rapidly raced to the doctor. Doctor Bannon was getting ready to leave for the night when they arrived at a fast pace. Terence quickly said," My sister is ill. Please help her." As he was helping her out of the buggy, Kara collapsed to the ground unconscious. Terence swooped her up in his arms. The doctor quickly opened the door. Doctor Bannon replied," Place your sister on the examining table." Terence asked," Is the Marshal in town?" Doctor Bannon opened the door to see Sheriff Micca patrolling the streets. She called out to him. When he walked up to her, she said," Go get my husband. Tell him to hurry." Shutting the door behind her,

Doctor Bannon started asking Terence questions. She placed a stethoscope on Kara's chest. Her heartbeat was faint. Marshal Bannon walked into the doctor's office. Terence said," It is I Terence in disguise. This is Kara. We are undercover. We were at the Marcello Winery today. Federico brought Kara to the Ma's Boarding House where we are staying. After he kissed her, she felt ill. Now she is out cold." Doctor Bannon placed smelling salts under her nose. Shortly thereafter she was awake. She looked at everyone. Stammering she said," This never happen before. I can't believe a simple kiss did this." Finally, she realized Marshal Bannon was standing there. She continued speaking in a strained tone of voice," Good, you are here. We have a problem. Federico told me he is selling everything to relocate to New York. We'll have to find the gems sooner than we planned." Marshal Bannon responded," He'll move the gems in the next shipment. The special bottles he uses to move the gems have an extra bottom attached to them and the bottles are a darker red. The regular wine bottle is a lighter red. Let's just say I received an anonymous tip. Did you order wine from him and where is it going?" Terence responded," I ordered 50 strawberry wine cases and 50 watermelon cases for a restaurant named Candlelight in New York." Doctor Bannon replied," Before you do anything, I need to make certain you can leave." Kara told everyone to give her and the doctor some privacy to figure out the cause of her fainting. Marshal Bannon and Terence stepped outside. After a thorough exam, Doctor Bannon called them in.

Kara said," I have an idea. We can tell Federico I have fallen ill from the exhausting trip and can't see him for a few days. This should give you time to find the gems. I can stay here under the good doctor's care." Marshal Bannon looked at them with skepticism. He wasn't sure the idea would work. Skeptically he asked," Doc, are you fine with going along with this ruse?" Doctor Bannon countered," She can stay for a few days at the clinic and I'll check on her thorough out the day. The fainting is puzzling. It could be from exhaustion, however, I won't rule out other possibilities." In a firm voice, Marshal Bannon said," You stay here, Terence. I have an idea where those gems possibly could be. Both of you being here, Federico will be distracted by coming to see you. Don't go overboard in pretending to be sick. He'll see through it and blow the cover off of us. I need the time to look at a few places." Terence told Doctor Bannon the undercover names they were using. They helped Kara into the room used by patients to recover from illness and surgery. Doctor Bannon gave her a nightgown she kept at the clinic for recovering patients. She changed out of her dress into the nightgown. When she was finally in bed, everyone left for the night.

The morning came with Francesa preparing to leave for New York. She had her trunk and duffle bags loaded on the carriage. Quizzically she asked Federico about his lunch date the day before. He told her about the large order of wine and the kiss with the beautiful lady. They finished breakfast before leaving for the train station in Pine Bluff. The carriage ride to the train station was pleasant for once. They chatted about the plans for their new life in New York. At the train station, Federico bid goodbye to his mother as she boarded the train. He observed the train go slowly down the track.

When Federico returned home, he immediately summoned Gin Bo. Before leaving Roaring Springs, there were a few things he wanted to settle. He didn't forget about being hit in the jaw by Cali Bannon. Marshal Bannon and Sheriff Micca did nothing about it. He was bitter about losing the property to the Diamond Rose Ranch. The ranch Cali Bannon owned with her family. The reservation was on the ranch's property to protect the Indians, another thing that annoyed him. He wanted to teach them a lesson about staying in your place. The Indian's place was in the ground. The woman's place was to get married and take care of the house. She shouldn't be ranching like a cowboy. He heard rumors about an outlaw that would take work from anybody willing to pay the price. He sent Gin Bo to find Dirty Birch Sayer. He wanted to hire him to take care of those who irritated him.

Next, Fedrico went to the warehouse to fill the order Noah Canton placed. He decided it would be a good cover to get the special bottles to New York under the disguise of this order. He saw Earl by the wagon. He shouted for Earl to come to him. When Earl walked up to him, Federico instructed him to load the special bottles with this shipment. Earl didn't like going to the cave nestled by the stream to get the special bottles. He would hear strange sounds that frighten him. He had a feeling someone was watching his every move. Nervously Earl stammered," I don't like going to that cave. It has strange sounds and feels like someone is watching." Federico snapped," I don't care what you think or feel. Those special bottles are in a cave on a property I do not own anymore. I want all those bottles removed today. Failure not to comply is not an option. Do you understand?" Clearing his throat, Earl stammered," I'll get it done." Federico retorted," Good, the order is one hundred bottles going to the Candlelight Restaurant in New York. When the wagons are loaded, ship the wine from the train station in Pine Bluff." Earl never understood why he didn't use the train from Roaring Springs. He knew not to ask. Federico had a temper that could be violent. Earl started on the first load of wine crates. Each crate had twelve bottles of wine. He knew one wagon could hold fifty crates stacked two high.

Federico had the carriage take him to Ma's Boarding house. May told him Arabella was at the doctor's office. He quickly went to the doctor's office. Doctor Bannon was at her desk when Federico walked in. They greeted each other with a hello. Federico softly asked," Is Arabella still here?" Doctor Bannon responded," Yes, you may see her for a few minutes. Please do not kiss her when you leave." Smiling, Federico said," I'll try not to." Doctor Bannon escorted him into the room. After Federico sat down in the chair by the bed, Doctor Bannon stepped out of the room, closing the door behind her. Kara started to sit up, but Federico told her to stay still. She softly said," After you kissed me, I fainted. I guess your kiss is powerful." Chuckling, he quipped," My kisses have been known to cause a few fainting ladies." They started to chat about New York. Shortly thereafter, he went to the jewelry store.

CHAPTER 06

While Smokin Peat was riding his horse to meet his men for another bank robbery, he rode into a grove. In the grove was a steep rock formation that had an opening slightly hidden among the trees. As he was riding past it, he overheard voices coming from the opening. He carefully turned his horse toward the trees. To his surprise, the voice he heard belonged to Dirty Birch, who was talking to a man with his back facing him. He thought it was a fluke he finally found Dirty Birch after giving up searching for him. He sat silently on his horse to try to listen in on the conversation. The man snapped," My employer wants Cali Bannon and the Indians dead. He doesn't care how you do it." Dirty Birch devilishly said," I'll take the women to the border. I'll get a good price for them." The man gave Dirty Birch money and a piece of paper as he retorted," This is the place you go to. He wants it done quickly." When the man turned toward Smokin Peat, he recognized the face as Gin Bo who worked for Federico. He waited for them to leave. They went in separate directions. He had an uneasy feeling he may not get there in time to warn them. When he met up with his men, he quickly told them to go ahead with the robbery without him, because he had something important to do first. He was hoping with each pounding hoof he would get there in time.

Marshal Bannon watched Federico leave the jewelry store. He decided to follow him. He used the side trails. He could easily watch them among the trees without being noticed. He observed him returning to the winery. It occurred to him he didn't see Francesca, Gin Bo, and her bodyguards today. He would usually see them coming and going out of the jewelry store. Gin Bo rarely was away from Federico. He started to wonder if they had left town. He returned to town to follow a hunch.

He saw Reverend Hollis coming from the church. Reverend Hollis was an older gentleman that loved everybody. The townspeople would do anything for him because of his kind spirit. Marshal Bannon rode up to him. Reverend Hollis happily said, " Good afternoon, Marshal. Is there something I can do for you?" Marshal Bannon replied," I didn't see Francesca today. Did you see her today?" Reverend Hollis responded," Yes, I did. It was yesterday afternoon. She told me goodbye because she was moving to New York permanently. She said she wanted to live again. I gave her my blessing of a safe journey. Is there something wrong?" Disappointed, Marshal Bannon said," No, I thank you." Marshal Bannon rode to the doctor's office to check on the patient.

Indian Agent, Joseph Silver, rode to the reservation to see Chief Eagle. He wanted to know if Chief Eagle decided to move to Oklahoma. Chief Eagle and the Indian Agent, Joseph Silver, sat around the fire talking about it. Wise Owl joined them in the discussion. The tribal elders would have to gather together to discuss it. Chief Eagle had Brave Hunter gather the elders for the special meeting. The meeting house was near Chief Eagle's house. It was the place where the tribal elders would meet with Chief Eagle. Before the tribal elders enter, Wise Owl would start a fire. The special stones were close to the fire for Wise Owl to put holy water on them by using a large spoon. This was done to clear the air of bad spirits and bring clear thoughts from the Great Spirit. Chief Eagle introduced Joseph to the tribal elders and Wise Owl. They sat around the fire ring discussing the journey to Oklahoma. The tribal elders listened intently to Joseph as he explained the importance of being with their people. They talked well into the night. They took turns voicing their opinions. Morning Star and Running Fawn voiced their concerns about the hardship on the women to make the journey, especially of those with children. By dawn's early light, the tribal elders and Chief Eagle agreed to go to Oklahoma. Joseph told them he would make the arrangements for them. He was relieved they agreed to go with him to Oklahoma. He thought it would be best for them. He would inform the Marshal once everything was ready for them to leave.

Running Fawn was disappointed upon hearing the news they were leaving. She accepted the decision with a smile. On the inside Running Fawn's heart was breaking. She mounted her horse to go for a ride. She rode toward the ranch. I saw Running Fawn riding toward me. I urged my horse into a trot to meet her halfway across the open range. When we stopped our horses, I saw the tears streaming down her face. She was upset about something. In a quivering voice, she said," We are leaving for Oklahoma. I don't want to leave. You are my best friend." I reached over and we hugged each other. I was saddened I was losing my best friend. I softly said," You're my best friend, too. I am going to miss you. Do you know when you will be leaving?" She took a breath and slowly let it out. She replied," I am not sure yet. The Indian Agent has to get things ready for us." Sitting back in my saddle, I responded," We can enjoy our time together until you leave. Do you feel up to a ride?" I knew a ride would help her feel a little better. She always enjoyed going on rides with me. In a low voice, she replied," I would like that." We always rode to the waterfall.

It is our favorite place to go. We decided to ride slowly today. The horses did a slow walk.

Gin Bo arrived at the winery. He saw Federico at the warehouse. He could tell by his actions he was irritated by something. Gin Bo said," Dirty Birch and his men will be here soon." In a gruff voice, Federico replied," Good, the sooner I get finished here, the sooner I can leave. Earl did not load the wagons. He left and the other workers followed him. They are afraid to go get the special bottles from the cave. You and I will have to load the wagons." Gin Bo took off his coat and rolled up his sleeves. By mid-afternoon, they had one wagon loaded with the regular wine bottle cases. They decided to take a break before going to the cave.

Emmet was eating at the café when Deputy Barixa offered to join him at his table. He didn't want to eat alone. Emmet was glad to have his company. They started talking about various topics. When Deputy Barixa started talking about the good fishing spot near Willow Creek, Emmet became interested. He was an avid fisherman. He felt he could use a short break from work. They agreed to go fishing after they finished eating.

Deputy Barixa and Emmet arrived at Willow Creek. They put the buckboard under a tree. They tied the horses to a branch. They carried their fishing poles and bait to the bank. They started catching the fish. Emmit was feeling relaxed. A gentle breeze rustled the leaves in the trees. The water softly rippled before him. Deputy Barixa told Emmet they'll have plenty of catfish for supper.

Gin Bo and Federico drove the freight wagon to the cave. The cases of wine were on boards and covered with canvas. The stream ran through the cave. Gin Bo stepped down from the wagon. He was still fighting exhaustion. He wanted more than anything to go to his room to rest. Federico jumped down from the wagon. They removed the canvas to start loading the cases of wine. The wind became stronger. The rippling of the stream became louder. They felt the ground trembling under their feet. They had a bad feeling something was going to happen. Gin Bo walked out of the cave. Upon seeing the spirit warriors, he ran back into the cave. The spirit warriors arrived in full force. They surrounded the cave. A long drawn out strong eerie voice dragged out the word, W-A-H-K-AN G-A-D-O-H-I! The voice repeated itself several times. Federico swallowed a lump in his throat. The spirit warriors screamed," AHIYALA!" Next, the spirit warriors started yelling blood-curling screams that sent chills down their spines. Gin Bo ran toward the rear entrance of the cave. His heart was pounding loudly with each step. It was getting difficult to breathe. He exited the cave to the grass clearing. In slow motion, he saw a spirit warrior riding his horse toward him. He became petrified.

The spirit warrior rode his horse through Gin Bo, causing him to drop to the ground. Federico watched the horse hitched to the wagon become unhitched. When the horses ran off, the wagon shattered into pieces. Federico was shaking with fear. His legs were like jello as he tried to run. He was horrified to see Gin Bo drop to the ground from the spirit warrior riding through him. Deputy Barixa and Emmet heard the ruckus. They dropped their fishing poles to go to the yelling. As they approached, Deputy Barixa thought he was hallucinating. Emmet froze in his tracks. They saw Gin Bo on the ground. Deputy Barixa closed his eyes for a brief second. He whispered to himself this is not real. He reopened his eyes to see Federico collapse to his knees. Federico looked like a ragged doll beaten to death. They watched him collapse to his side. Suddenly Deputy Barixa fainted. Emmet finally found the courage to run. His body was shaking with fear as he ran down the road repeatedly screaming," Help me!" The ranch hands Webb and Rusty were searching for calves that wandered off during pasture rotation. Running Fawn and I returned from our ride. We heard Emmet screaming. We immediately urged our horses in a gallop.

When we approached, Emmet dropped to his knees. In a ragged breath, he stammered," They're dead. Indians... Spirits...Cave." Rusty replied," I'll go get the doctor and the Marshal." I quickly dismounted. Emmet passed out. Webb removed his canteen from his saddle as he dismounted. While Rusty galloped to town, Running Fawn decided to get Wise Owl And Spirit Dancer. I put my jacket under Emmet's head. Webb took off his bandana from around his neck. He poured water from the canteen onto the bandana. He patted Emmet's face with the wet bandana. Running Fawn returned with Spirit Dancer and Wise Owl. Emmet slowly opened his eyes. I gently asked," Emmet, could you tell us what happened?" Emmet stammered," I was... we were fishing. Deputy Barixa and me heard yelling. We took...a look by the cave up the stream. Spirit Indians... riding horses. Two men... I don't know... fell to the ground after spirit Indians rode through...them. Deputy Barixa collapsed to the...ground. I a...ran." Wise Owl softly said," The Spirit Warriors came. They did not harm you or your friend. We must go see why they were angry." We heard horses coming. We were glad to see it was my pa and ma. Rusty was riding beside my pa. Doctor Bannon rapidly dismounted with the medical bag in her hand. She could tell by her appearance hew was in shock. She ordered Webb and Rusty to take him to the ranch's main house. I informed my pa what Emmet told us. Marshal Bannon carefully said," Wise Owl, Spirit Dancer, I need to go see what happened. I'll need your help with the spirit warriors."

Wise Owl replied," As I have told you before, we can not control the spirits. When they are angry, there is a reason. We'll ask the Great Spirit to help us." Marshal Bannon, Wise Owl, Spirit Dancer, Running Fawn, and I carefully rode to the cave. We saw them on the ground and the shattered wagon. Running Fawn and I rode up to Deputy Barixa. Marshal Bannon, Wise Owl, and Spirit Dancer dismounted from their horses. The wind was calm. The water in the stream flowed softly. It was quiet and peaceful.

Marshal Bannon checked Federico for any sign of life. He was gone. Next, Doctor Bannon came driving a buckboard with Webb and Rusty. Doctor Bannon went to Gin Bo. She did not find a pulse or a heartbeat. He was dead, too. Deputy Barixa staggered to his feet. We helped him to the buckboard. Doctor Bannon went to Federico. Marshal said," He is dead, too. I'll notify his mother." Webb and Rusty carried Gin Bo and Federico bodies to the buckboard. Marshal Bannon opened a wine case. He removed a bottle of wine. He noticed the false bottom. Carefully removing the bottom, he saw the black pouch inside. After he put the bottle down, he opened the pouch, revealing the gems. He told Webb to go get another wagon. Doctor Bannon examined deputy Barixa, who was still shaking. Marshal Bannon asked," Wise Owl, Spirit Dancer, could you explain to me about the spirit warriors? I was on the sacred ground before with Sheriff Micca without you, and the spirit warriors didn't come. Emmet and Barixa went fishing here, and they are fine except for being rattled by what they saw." Spirit Dancer softly replied," The spirit warriors know a good person from bad. You were not harmed because they see a good man." Wise Owl responded," Emmet and Deputy Barixa were only fishing and meant no harm. They can fish and the spirit warriors will not harm them. To walk on wahkan gadohi your heart must be pure. The spirit warriors saw the two who died had darkness in their souls. The spirit warriors protect the innocent, the defenseless from those who want to harm them." Frowning, Marshal Bannon said," I have to admit the spirit warriors were right. They were the jewelry thieves I was hoping to catch." Webb came with a wagon. A dozen cases of wine were quickly loaded. Once the cases were loaded, they went to town. Running Fawn and I gathered the fishing poles. We put them in Deputy Barixa's wagon. I overheard the conversation about the healing ceremony.

Wise Owl and Spirit Dancer decided to do a healing ceremony to perhaps lay the spirit warriors to rest. Running Fawn and I offered to help gather the stones to create the sacred circle. I asked," Why are circles a part of the ceremonies?" I was curious about the importance of circles they seem to require to do certain things. Spirit Dancer answered," A circle has no end. Life is sacred and no one has the right to take another life. The Sacred Circle creates healing, peace, unity, and harmony for all life. We ask the Great Spirit to guide us on our journey in the Sacred Circle." Wise Owl put special stones in the middle of the fire ring before he lit the fire. Spirit Dancers splashed the stones with water from a large wooden spoon. As the steam rose from the drench stones, Wise Owl look upward with his arms and hands stretched out. He gently said," Great Spirit, heal the wounded souls by giving them peace. Great Spirit, heal their hurt, and may their journey on Mother Earth come to final rest. Aho."

Terence was sitting with Kara when they walked into the clinic. Doctor Bannon asked Rusty and Webb to escort, Emmet, to a recovery room. Marshal Bannon escorted Deputy Barixa to another room. She said," They'll need to rest a few days." Marshal Bannon walked up to Kara. He said," I hope you're feeling better because I have something to show you the two of you at my office."

Marshal Bannon walked out of the clinic to go to his office. Webb and Rusty unloaded the wine cases into his office. Next, Marshal Bannon made a telephone call to Marcello Winery in New York. When he asked the person on the other line to speak to Francesca Marcello, he was told she had died unexpectedly that morning. He proceeded to inform them about Federico. The person told him his Uncle Lucas would come to bring Federico to be buried by his mother in New York. He hung up the telephone. Terence and Kara were standing in his office. Marshal Bannon had Webb give him a bottle of wine. He showed Terence and Kara the false bottom and sack of hidden gems inside. They were surprised to see the false bottom. They thought it was a clever way to hide the gems. Marshal Bannon informed them about Francesca and Federico Marcello. Terence asked," May I use your telephone to call our office?" Marshal Bannon permitted him. At the Pinkerton office, Terence requested to speak to his boss. Upon hearing his boss's voice, Terence informed him about the events that had occurred. His boss told him the jewel carrier, Kye Thorn who had business dealings with the Marcellos, had passed away during questioning. A tip led to them apprehending him at the train station. They recovered a folder with a secret compartment to hide the gems. The doctor tested the special wine Kye Thorn had at his house. The doctor discovered the special wine had deadly bacteria from the water used to make it. He informed his boss they would be returning to New York with the remaining missing gems by the end of the week. After he hung up the telephone, Terence said," Marshal, Kye Thorn, Marcello's jewel dealer died from drinking the special wine. The doctor's tested the wine found at his house. They discovered it is tainted with deadly bacteria from the water being used to make it." Kara replied," It could be the reason I became sick. I sipped the special wine with Federico before going to Ma's Boarding House." Marshal Bannon responded," I'll have Doctor Bannon check this wine." They removed the gems from the false bottoms of the wine bottles. Kara said," I'll go get the lockbox from my room. I don't want the gems to get lost along the way." While she went to get the lockbox, Terence and Marshal Bannon looked at the small sacks of diamonds, rubies, and emeralds. When Kara returned with the lockbox, they signed the voucher slip to verify the gems were accounted for. Terence said," We'll be leaving in the morning. We thank you for your help, Marshal." Kara locked the lockbox. She'll hide it in her trunk to make it safer to travel. Marshal Bannon took the bottle of special wine to Doctor Bannon.

At the clinic, Doctor Bannon was busy addressing Emmet's anxiety. Deputy Barixa was slowly calming down. Marshal Bannon put the bottle on

her desk. She walked out of Emmet's room. Seeing the bottle, she asked,"
What is the bottle of wine for?" He answered," The Pinkerton's were told
about the wine being tainted. Francesca Marcello and their jewel dealer
have died from it. A doctor in New York discovered a deadly bacteria in
the wine." Doctor Bannon removed the cork. The wine had a very strong
vinegar odor that offended their noses. Doctor Bannon responded," This
wine is bad. You can tell by the smell. I'll test it to see if there are bacteria
in it." She poured a small amount of wine into a glass. She used a slide and
eye dropper to test it under the microscope. Peering into the microscope,
she said," The wine has bacteria in it. I think it would be best we test the
water in the stream, Willow Creek, and the wells at the winery." Marshal
Bannon replied," I'll go get the water samples for you." She responded,"
I'll give you the sample jars to collect the water. Mark each bottle where
you collect the water. Once the source of bacteria is found, we can seal off
the water." He picked up the test jars as he said," Federico's uncle will be
coming to take his body to New York. I'll let the undertaker know as I leave
town. I'll be back as soon as I can."

When I was leaving the ranch, my pa stopped by to ask me to help him
gather water samples. We rode to the winery first. We looked around for
the wells. I came upon an above-ground spring with a pipe sticking out of
the bank with rocks. The water flowed to a stone pool to contain the water
below. I put the jar into the water. I noticed a sign stating SPECIAL WINE
ONLY. Marshal Bannon gathered water samples from the three wells found
at the winery. Next, we took samples from the stream and Willow Creek.
We marked each jar as we took the samples. The next step was to give the
jars to Doctor Bannon.

Doctor Bannon was ready for us when we walked in with the jars. I
said," Ma, this one jar is from a spring with a sign in front of it saying
special wine." She tested the jar first. She placed a few drops of water on

the slide. Looking at the sample carefully, she replied," This water is the source of the bacteria. It is bad water." She tested the remaining samples as a precaution. The other samples of water were clear of the bacteria. Marshal Bannon responded," They were using bad water and didn't know it. I'll put up a sign by the spring to warn people it's bad water. All the special wine will be destroyed. I'll put a notice out in the paper to warn the public that if they have the special wine to not drink it because it's tainted." Marshal Bannon swiftly went to see Dottie about putting the notice in the afternoon edition.

The excitement of the day was starting to wind down. I returned to the ranch with the evening sun setting. I saw Charlie and Henry were busy. They were preparing super for the hands. Their chit-chat among themselves filled the air. They decided to eat outside. They gathered around the tables as Charlie and Herny filled their plates of fried chicken, potatoes, and biscuits. Charlie made a treat for the hands. He decided to make ice tea to drink with their super. The hands enjoyed the cool drink. Henry placed pieces of ice in the pitcher. The ranch had its own ice house and smokehouse. I heard Charlie call my name. I gave him a wave. He motioned for me to join them. I walked over to a table. Webb gave me a chair to sit down. A plate of food and a glass of ice tea was placed before me. We chatted about the day as we ate.

The Pinkerton's left on the morning train. Judge Ward remained in town to assist Indian Agent Joseph Silver with the process of having the Cherokee relocate to the reservation in Oklahoma. They wanted the transition to go smoothly as possible. The train would only let them use the boxcars to transport the Cherokee. The livestock car would transport their horses. Next, Marshal Bannon was told by Indian Agent Joseph Silver the arrangements were made for the Cherokee to go to the reservation within a week. He and Marshal Bannon rode to the reservation to inform Chief Eagle about the arrangements.

My hands and I were mending fences when I saw them riding toward the reservation. I decided to follow them. Chief Eagle greeted them with a wave of his hand. I rode up to my pa. I listened to Indian Agent Silver say," Chief Eagle, the arrangements were made for you and your people to take the train to Oklahoma within a week. You and your people will be riding in the boxcars. Your horses will be transported by livestock car. I'll be riding the boxcar with you. I'll personally see to it the move go smoothly." I replied," I'll have my hands bring wagons over to help with the move." Marshal Bannon responded," I'll see to it you and your people are left alone for you to leave peacefully." Chief Eagle shook our hands to thank us for our help. I could hear a quiver in his voice as Chief Eagle said," It is with great sadness I have to leave. Perhaps someday we can all live in harmony with each other. I thank you Wil and Cali for your friendship." We watched him walk up to Wise Owl and Spirit Dancer. He asked them to do a prayer for all of them to have a safe journey to their new place. He had the women begin to get ready for the move. The men started to prepare the horses. I rode to the ranch to gather the wagons to help them. I had my hands drive the wagons over to the reservation to begin loading with the women's help.

I saw Running Fawn and a few other women by the creek. They were checking the fish traps to make lunch. I urged my horse into a slow trot. I rode up to them. After I dismounted, I helped them gather the traps.

Before going to the reservation, Dirty Birch had to find more men for the raid. Gin Bo paid him a large sum of money to do the job. His brother agreed to help him. The men they found at the saloons were rough and rowdy that worked for the highest bidder. They took the money with no questions asked. Most of the men riding with him had prior run-ins with the law. They agreed to take the women to the border to be sold. They were getting closer to the reservation with each minute of pounding hooves.

Dirty Birch Sayer thrived on being mean, cruel, and violent. At the brutal hands of his drunken father, he learned to be cruel. His father was in a drunken rage when he killed his mother. She had woken him for supper. The bottle he threw at her hit her in the head. He and his brother ran away. They grew up hard, fast with a gun, and nasty. Their father died in a drunken brawl at a saloon a few years later.

CHAPTER 07

Moon Beam was near my horse. She was a young child who enjoyed horses. I picked her up to put her in the saddle. She was delighted to be riding my horse. We started carrying the fish traps to the fire. Suddenly there was chaos all around us. Dirty Birch had arrived with his men shooting at anything that moved. I told Moon Beam to ride for help. Her heart was racing as she urged my horse in a gallop. She knew she had to get to Tin Star. I screamed," Morning Star, you and the women take cover!" I was dodging bullets and returning fire. I could hear screams from men, women, and children crying. Marshal Bannon was trying to fight them. My hands were shooting back with their rifles. Smokin Peat arrived firing his pistols. When he saw Running Fawn collapse to the ground from being shot across the forehead, he had his horse gallop toward her. At that very moment, Dirty Birch grabbed Running Fawn. Dirty Birch flung her across his saddle as he rode away. Smokin Peat saw him leave with Running Fawn. A rage swiftly swept through him. He had his horse go in a fast gallop after Dirty Birch. As the outlaws fled, they grabbed a few women. Marshal Bannon had his horse go into a gallop as he raced after them. Moon Beam arrived with Sheriff Micca and his deputies following behind him. They instantly rode after Marshal Bannon once I told them which direction he was going. Doctor Bannon came with Deputy Barixa riding beside her. She quickly started treating the wounded. I had a few scrapes on my left arm from dodging bullets behind the tree. The place was in shambles.

Smokin Peat was hot on the heels of Dirty Birch. He wanted to save Running Fawn from him. He chased after him. Fortunately, Dirty Birch's horse lost its footing going down an embankment. Dirty Birch went flying off the saddle sideways. Running Fawn came to rest in a ditch. When Dirty Birch reached for his gun, Smokin Peat shot him in the chest. Next, Smokin Peat dismounted. He carefully picked up Running Fawn. She was still unconscious. He gently placed her on his saddle. He carefully mounted his horse. He sat on the saddle behind her. He held her close to him with one arm. While holding the reins in the other hand, he nudged the horse in a slow trot to his cabin.

Upon arriving at his cabin, he carried her inside. He noticed the graze across her forehead had not stopped bleeding. He delicately laid her down on the bed. He covered her with a quilt. He used a bedsheet from a trunk at the foot of the bed to make bandages. He put water in a washbasin to clean her wound. After her wound was cleaned, he went to get honey to put on it.

When he returned to the cabin with the honey and two rabbits he shot, he placed the honey on her wound and then bandage it. Next, he started to make stew. He grew his vegetables behind the cabin. He learned from his ma about canning vegetables to keep from starving to death in the winter months. He started a fire in the fireplace. He watched her slowly breathe. He was hoping she would open her eyes soon. He ate at the table in silence. He was wondering if he should go for help. After he finished eating, he placed a chair by the bed. He sat down, waiting patiently. She started to move her arms. She was trying to get up. She fell back down in the bed. He quickly went to her. He gently said," Stay still. You were hurt. Can you eat? Are you thirsty?" She let out a sigh as she said," I am hungry and thirsty. How did you find me?" He made her a plate of stew and a cup of water. He helped her sit up in bed. She slowly ate her stew. He softly replied," When I saw men attacking your village, I joined Cali to help fight them off. I saw you dropping to the ground. Before I could get to you, Dirty Birch scooped you up on a horse and rode away with you. I went after you. Dirty Birch's horse stumbled. He fell off his horse. You fell into a ditch. He reached for his gun and I shot him. I picked you up and brought you here." She finished eating. He put the plate and cup in the sink. He helped her to lay down. She softly asked," Would you hold me?" Not saying a word, he laid down beside her. He wrapped his arms around her. She laid her head on his chest. She felt safe in his arms. She drifted off to sleep.

In the morning, she awoke with a headache. He could tell by the facial expression she was in severe pain. She gripped his hand. She said," Peat, I need you to make willow bark tea for my pain." He softly whispered," I'll go get you some. Just relax until I return." He gently kissed her on the cheek. His kiss felt soothing to her. He quietly left the cabin to get her willow bark. When he returned with it, she told him how to make the tea. After she finished drinking her tea, he made them breakfast. She beginning to feel better. She said," I know nothing about you. Tell me about your life. Do you have a last name?" He sat down on the chair. He was running from the law and his past. He let out a sigh. He replied," My full name is Peat Jeremiah Calbert. My pa was a dirt poor farmer. Ma tried to make it the best life she good. She taught me about the honey on the wounds. I had a bad scrape from a tree. She put honey on it because we couldn't pay a doctor. Pa died working the fields in the hot sun. Ma passed the following Spring from a sickness that the doctor couldn't cure. I survived the sickness. The doctor took a dozen of eggs for payment. The bank took the farm. Penniless, I robbed banks and stagecoaches. The law is looking for me. I had a girl once, but she left me. I didn't believe she would leave me. I came home to find a note on the table. She was gone for good and didn't want to see me anymore. I am called Smokin Peat because my gun smokes." He paused for a moment to choose his words carefully. She sat up in bed. She saw the sadness in his eyes. He sat down beside her on the bed. He took her hands into his. He gently said," Running Fawn, I have loved you from the moment we met. You were so beautiful standing in the meadow. I promise I'll never hurt you. I'll live an honest life. Come with me, we can go anywhere." He stopped talking to give her a quick kiss on the lips before he finished speaking," As long we're together, that's all that matters to me." She placed her hand on his cheek. Her heart fluttered when he kissed her. She wasn't expecting it. He noticed her surprised expression. Turning red with embarrassment he replied," I'm sorry. I got a little carried away." She gently said," Peat, I see goodness in your eyes. I feel the same way. I would like to go with you, but I can not live in your world. You can not live in mine. I have to go to my people. My family is looking for me. Please, take me to them." Peat knew she was right. She had a family to return to. Even though it meant losing her forever, he agreed to take her home. He softly said," You get some rest. We'll leave first thing in the morning." Before he stood up, she kissed him on his lips. She said," Thank you for understanding." He softly touched her cheek. He started to get ready for the journey home. Peat knew in his heart he had to return Running Fawn to her people.

The following day they left the cabin to begin the journey home. Peat was taking his time. A slow but steady walking pace. They rode together on his horse. He did his best to take trails less rocky. In a way, he was delaying the time to return Running Fawn by taking the longer smoother trails. Being night was coming upon them, they stop to make camp. After they dismounted, Peat went to gather firewood. Running Fawn laid out the bedrolls. She was torn in two. One part of her wanted to stay with Peat and the other part wanted to be with her family. This will be their last night together. She was going to cherish every moment of it. Peat returned with the firewood. Once the fire was going, she made them biscuits and bacon with coffee. The stars began to appear. She told him about them leaving for Oklahoma. They quietly sat beside each other. Neither knew what to say. She was going far away and there was nothing he could do to stop it. She broke the silence by asking him to hold her one last time. He slid his arms around her waist. She leaned her head against her chest. Beneath the pale moonlight, he softly kissed her sweet cherry lips by the crackling fire. Their hearts were pounding with a burning fever that was getting stronger. The yearning to touch was something they couldn't deny any longer. Her hands were like velvet as she slip his shirt off. He gently lowered her dress while he caressed her body. Their bodies were quivering with each touch. As he nibbled on her neck, he ever so tenderly held her close to him. She felt his muscular bare chest against her bosom. Tingling sensations swept through them like wildfire. They felt their souls touch. They melted into each other's arms. Body to body they became one.

The half dozen outlaws who took Morning Star, Yellow Feather, Graceful Doe, and Singing Tree were having a difficult night. Morning Star, Yellow Feather, Graceful Doe, and Singing Tree were praying the Great Spirit would rescue them. The spirit warriors made their presence known. An outlaw came too close to Morning Star. He reached out to touch her arm to pull her closer to him. His hand felt a force preventing him from touching her. Suddenly he was being thrown into the trees away from her. He landed on the ground hard. The other outlaw drew his pistol. He shouted," Show yourself!" The pistol in his hand became extremely hot. Screaming in pain, he immediately dropped the gun. His hand was burning. The remaining outlaws drew their pistols and demanded the person show themself. The wind blew their campfire out. This made the outlaws angrier. A lightning flash gave them a glimpse of the spirit warriors coming toward them. They felt a sudden rush of something they never felt before. Another clap of lightning showed the spirits warriors surrounding them. When the outlaws tried to use their guns, the triggers broke. Fear swept through them. Once they heard the blood-curling screams with no one in sight, they swiftly ran. The rope binding Morning Star, Yellow Feather, Graceful Doe, and Singing Tree's hands fell off. They took the two horses near the tree. Riding double, they rode away.

Dawn's early light, Sheriff Micca and his deputies found Morning Star, Yellow Feather, Graceful Doe, and Singing Tree riding toward them. They were surprised they were able to get free. The women told them the best they could the direction the outlaws may have taken. Sheriff Micca insisted a deputy escort the women to their village. He and the remaining deputies continued after the outlaws.

Marshal Bannon and I were searching for Running Fawn. We found Dirty Birch dead. We decided to ride in separate directions. We agreed to shoot twice if we found Running Fawn. I rode into a grove of trees. Smokin Peat and Running Fawn saw my horse. They trotted their horses to me. I was relieved to see her. When we stopped our horses, we dismounted. We gave each other hugs. I happily said," I'm glad you're safe. Smokin Peat, good job." Running Fawn replied," Peat, I think it would be best I go with Cali." I stepped back to give them privacy to say their goodbyes. Peat responded," It would be best. I don't want to see the Marshal. I would have to explain to him how I rescued you. I don't think he would understand I did it because I loved you." She softly whispered," I love you, too. In my heart, you will always be." They hugged and passionately kissed. He held her tightly against him. He wanted to hold her forever. He softly whispered in her ear," I love you Running Fawn. You'll be in my heart forever." Another long passionate kiss and warm embrace, he let her go. For a brief second, she laid her hand on his chest. They looked into each other's eyes. Silently, she walked toward me. Their hearts were breaking. Running Fawn and I rode together out of the grove. He watched her ride away, taking his heart with her. I fired two shots to signal my pa. Marshal Bannon heard the two shots. He turned his horse around at a gallop. Running Fawn took off her bandage around her head. I said," Put it in my saddlebag. I'll get rid of it later. My ma will look at your forehead when we get home." Marshal Bannon rode up to us. Smiling, he said," Glad to see you. Cali, take Running Fawn to your ma first. She should have that cut on her forehead checked." We rode together to the reservation.

Doctor Bannon stayed at the reservation to attend to those injured during the raid. Wise Owl and Spirit Dancer assisted. They were happy everyone returned safely. Doctor Bannon looked at Running Fawn's forehead. The cut needed a few stitches. Indian Agent Silver was stunned about the raid. He looked around the shambled mess. Marshal Bannon walked up to him. After Doctor Bannon finished stitching Running Fawn's cut, she walked toward them. She said," In a few days they'll be able to travel. Perhaps they will be able to live in peace there." Marshal Bannon responded," Let's hope they can. I never understood the need to pick on someone different." Indian Agent Silver replied," I don't know, either. We can all learn from each other to live in peace. Why do you think they attacked?" Marshal Bannon answered," The women are worth money at the border." Morning Star approached them. She said," When we prayed to the Great Spirit to help us, the spirit warriors came. They made the bad men run away. We saw the horses near the tree. We rode until we saw Tin Star. I don't think he'll find the bad men. The Great Spirit will take of them." She turned to see her daughter. She continued speaking," I am grateful the Great Spirit was watching over my daughter." Running Fawn walked up to her mother. Together, they went to see Chief Eagle. The process of preparing to leave continued with those who were able. The ranch hands repaired the wagons that were overturned. The horses were rounded up. I listened to Morning Star talking about the spirit warriors. I thought Wise Owl and Spirit Dancer did a healing prayer to lay them to rest. I was pondering about this when Spirit Dancer approached me. She asked," Cali, are you puzzled about something?" I replied," Yes, I was trying to understand about the spirit warriors. I thought you and Wise Owl did a healing ceremony for them to rest in peace. But, then I heard Morning Star talk about them. They recused them." Spirit Dancer motioned for me to follow her. We walked to the creek. After we sat down under a tree, she responded," The spirit warriors protect the innocent. The Great Spirit sends them. Each of us has spirits watching over us. We can not see them, but they are there. They help guide us on our journey in life." I replied," It is similar to what we call angels. They are there when we need them." Smiling, she responded," Sometimes a person listens to the wrong spirit. They become lost. For them to get on the right path, they come to us to help guide them. Some chose to stay in the darkness. They believe the wrong spirit strongly. Sometimes they change before it's too late." She made sense to me. The spirits and angels were the same, only different names. Spirit Dancer and I walked to the wagons to help to load.

By evening the wagons were finally loaded. The horses were ready. One more day before they were to leave. Everyone was exhausted with the packing and clean-up from the raid. We sat around the fire remembering the good times. The hunting trips, weddings, and births were many happier times. There was sadness in the air. How do we let go of friends that we had known most of our life? I didn't have the answer. It was as though someone had ripped my heart out of me. Running Fawn and I would go for long rides. There was something about riding horses that made us forget the time. We shared laughter and tears. It was coming to an end. I was holding back the tears until I was alone. Perhaps this was a dream and I'll wake up to see my friend still here.

The following morning Sheriff Micca and his deputies brought in the remaining outlaws. Marshal Bannon observed them coming into town. The deputies quickly put them in jail. Sheriff Micca rode up to Marshal Bannon. He said," Wil, I need the Doc to look at a hand. They told me the gun burned the hand, and they saw warriors attacking them. You wouldn't believe the wild story they told me." Grinning, Marshal Bannon replied, " I believe it. Morning Star told me all about it. I'll get Doc for you." With a nod and tilt of the hat, Sheriff Micca rode over to his office. Marshal Bannon approached Doctor Bannon at the café. She was having coffee with Dottie, who wrote about the raid.

Marshal Bannon told her about the prisoner needing medical attention at Sheriff Micca's jail. She went to her clinic to get her medical bag. Dottie came with her. Next, they went to see the prisoner. The outlaws were shabby in appearance. They rattled on about the warriors appearing out of nowhere. Doctor Bannon treated the burned hand. The other outlaw complained about his back and arm pain.

When he told her he was thrown into a tree, she looked at Sheriff Micca. He said," I am not sure what happened to them before we found them hiding in an old abandoned shack." She replied," His back is badly bruised, but his arm is broken. I'll need to set it and splint it." Judge Ward walked into the jail with Marshal Bannon. He said," Being I am here, I'll give them a fair trial. Doc, when can they be tried for their crime?" Before she could answer, the outlaws in unison said," We are guilty. We confess we did it. We don't want to leave this jail." The one gruff-looking outlaw said," We are safer in here. We'll take our time." Judge Ward responded,"

Very well when your ready to be processed, Marshal Bannon and Sheriff Micca will begin the proceedings." After she finished setting the arm, the deputy locked the jail door. They had a feeling they knew what happened, but no one said anything about it.

The dreaded day came for Running Fawn and her people to leave. I couldn't understand the unfairness of life. I could come, go and live anywhere I choose. But my best friend could not. The government told them what to do because they were different. I did not understand why couldn't they have the same freedoms as I did. I truly wished things were different. I wished they could stay and be free to live out their lives peacefully. Chief Eagle and my pa were talking. Morning Star and my ma exchanged gifts. The ranch hands drove the wagons to the train station. Indian Agent Silver was at the station waiting for them. Their horses were loaded on a livestock car. Their belongings were placed in the boxcar. Running Fawn and I stood near the boxcar. As Marshal Bannon shook Chief Eagle's hand, he said," Go in peace, my friend." Chief Eagle replied," You have been a good friend. May the Great Spirit keep you safe." Morning Star and Doctor Bannon hugged. Neither knew what to say. The tears in their eyes spoke for them. Another quick hug and Morning Star boarded the boxcar with her people. Chief Eagle boarded the boxcar next. I softly said, " Running Fawn, I don't want to say goodbye. Perhaps, someday we'll see each other again." The tears were flowing from our eyes. Sadly, she replied," My dear friend, we do not say goodbye. We say, donadagohvi. It means till we meet again. Remember we are spirit sisters." As we hugged, I whispered," Spirit sisters forever." One more hug, then she joined her parents on the boxcar. The train whistle blew. The train started slowly rolling down the track. The hardest thing I ever had to do was watch my friend leave. It broke my heart. I used my bandana to wipe the tears from my eyes. I took a breath and then let it out slowly. I decided to go for a long ride.

When I mounted my horse, I rode to the meadow. Running Fawn's favorite place to pick wildflowers. I stopped my horse in the middle of the meadow. My thoughts about Running Fawn were interrupted by Smokin Peat. He had a shattered look. His voice quivered as he asked," Did she go to Oklahoma?" I softly replied," Yes, they left this morning." After he cleared his throat from a lump that wouldn't go down, he responded," I'll go to Oklahoma, too. I can't be her husband, but I can watch over her. I'll buy a spread near her." I quizzically asked," Did you shoot Dirty Birch Sayer?" Shifting in his saddle he answered," I did. Why do you ask?" I replied," Dirty Birch Sayer was worth $1,000.00 dead or alive. You can collect the reward. The money would give you a fresh start in Oklahoma. You could buy a spread near her." He thought about it for a moment. He asked," Would you go with me to see the Marshal?" I answered," I can, and if we go now, you can get started on your trip." Nodding in agreement, we rode to town.

Marshal Bannon was in his office when we walked in. I said," Pa, this is Smokin Peat. He's the one who shot Dirty Birch Sayer." Marshal Bannon looked at Smokin Peat as he asked," Tell me, How did it happen and where did it take place?" Smokin Peat firmly answered," He took Running Fawn. She was out cold. His horse lost its footing going down an embankment at Red Canyon. He fell off with Running Fawn. When he went to shoot, I shot him in the chest." Marshal Bannon pulled the bottom drawer of his desk open. He removed a cash box. After he unlocked the lid, he opened the box. Marshal Bannon asked," What are you going to use the money for?" Smokin Peat replied," I'm buying a spread far away from here." Marshal Bannon counted the money. Next, he had Smokin Peat sign a paper verifying he received the reward and the statement about Dirty Birch Sayer being dead was correct. As Marshal Bannon handed Smokin Peat the money, he responded," I hope you have a safe trip to where ever it is your going."

Marshal Bannon couldn't shake the feeling Smokin Peat looked familiar to him. He remembered looking at the wanted posters of the kissing bandit. It was a drawing of a man with a bandana over his face and wearing a hat. It was Smokin Peat's eyes that resembled the kissing bandit eyes in the wanted poster. Marshal Bannon shrugged it off. He couldn't question or arrest someone based on eye similarities. Smokin Peat stuff the money in his pocket. I said," Smokin Peat, I wish you the best of luck and hope you find the peace you're seeking." After he shook our hands, Smokin Peat left.

Smokin Peat rode to his cabin. He stuffed some clothes in a saddlebag. Then he walked to the barn. At the last stall, he removed a few boards from the stall floor. Underneath the stall floor were two sacks of gold nuggets. He remembered the old man that gave him the nuggets for protecting his mine from claim jumpers. When summer came, the old man paid him with the two sacks of nuggets. As the old man was leaving with his share of nuggets to a warmer and drier climate, he made Smokin Peat promise he would buy a farm and settle down. Once Smokin Peat found this cabin, he hid the nuggets until he was ready to quit being an outlaw and settle down. He put the two sacks of nuggets in his saddlebag. He began his journey to Oklahoma.

When Smokin Peat finally arrived at Stone Ridge, Oklahoma, he was glad to take a break from riding. He rode up to the Sheriff's office. He asked the grizzled Sheriff was the town close to the Cherokee reservation. The Sheriff told him the town border on the reservation. Next, he asked about land for sale. The Sheriff sent him to the land office at the end of town. Upon seeing the bank by the feed mill, Smokin Peat rode to the bank first. After dismounting, he removed the two sacks of gold from his saddlebag. The teller was a polite young man. Smokin Peat put the two sacks of gold on the counter. The bank manager was an older man with a beard. Smokin Peat asked," Could I cash the gold nuggets here?" The bank manager replied," I can help you with it. If you like, I can create an account for you to keep your money here." Smokin Peat responded," It would be fine." The bank manager filled the papers out for Smokin Peat and then weighed the gold nuggets. He gave Smoking Peat a slip verifying the deposit. Smokin Peat signed his account papers.

When he left the bank, he rode to the land office. The office clerk was a pleasant young man. When Smokin Peat asked him about land for sale, the clerk told him about a ranch. The rancher was selling because his ranch bordered the reservation, and he didn't want to live near the Cherokee. The clerk gave Smokin Peat directions to the ranch.

Smokin Peat found the circle T ranch. He rode up to the house. An older couple was greeted him at the door. Smokin Peat introduced himself and told him he would like to buy the ranch. The older couple looked at him in disbelief. The old man quizzically said," You don't mind living by those savages." Smokin Peat refrained from showing his anger. He didn't like the remark the old man said. He carefully replied," I don't mind. I want to buy a ranch to settle down. I have been drifting from town to town all over the place. I thought it was time I find a nice spread." The old woman responded," Rex, let's take him on the offer before he changes his mind." The old man said," I'll sell you everything. You'll get the livestock, tools, and a farmhand. The ranch is five hundred acres and has produced good crops every year." Smokin Peat and the older couple agreed to the price.

After they loaded the wagon of their possessions, they rode to town to transfer the deed to Smokin Peat. He told the land clerk the ranch's new name was "Wild Flowers". Once the deed was transferred, he rode to the Indian Agents office. He noticed the office riding to the ranch. Indian Agent Silver was sitting at his desk when he walked in. They greeted each other. Smokin Peat asked," Do you need a beef contract for the Cherokee reservation?" Indian Silver was surprised he asked about a beef contract.

The local ranchers were not willing to sell their beef to him. He had to have beef cows sent in from other places. Indian Agent Silver answered," I could use a local beef supplier. I'll draw up the contract and your name sir." Smokin Peat responded," My name is Peat Calbert. The ranch I own is Wild Flowers." He agreed by signing the contract to supply the Cherokee reservation one hundred head of beef cattle. He returned to the ranch feeling peaceful.

He rode around the property. He found a high ridge with stones and clusters of trees. A perfect view of the Cherokee village. He could observe them from above out of their sight. Even though it was evening, he saw Running Fawn talking with her mother by the creek. He would keep his distance. She would never know he was there watching over her. He would love her from a distance.

THE END

Made in United States
Orlando, FL
01 March 2022